# LOVE IN A MIST

Minnie Hyde — flame-haired beauty and acclaimed actress of her day — leaves a legacy of confusion when she dies without a will. Penny Graham, a single parent running a pet-grooming parlour in a disused theatre on the land, is soon threatened with eviction by Minnie's grandson, Roger Oakes. That is, until long-lost Australian granddaughter Sarah Deeds also lays claim to the estate. Amidst the confusion, Penny must deal with her growing feelings for a man who would make her homeless . . .

*Books by Margaret Mounsdon*
*in the Linford Romance Library:*

THE MIMOSA SUMMER
THE ITALIAN LAKE
LONG SHADOWS
FOLLOW YOUR HEART
AN ACT OF LOVE
HOLD ME CLOSE
A MATTER OF PRIDE
SONG OF MY HEART
MEMORIES OF LOVE
WRITTEN IN THE STARS
MY SECRET LOVE
A CHANCE ENCOUNTER
SECOND TIME AROUND
THE HEART OF THE MATTER
LOVE TRIUMPHANT
NIGHT MUSIC
FIT FOR LOVE
THE POWER OF LOVE
THE SWALLOW HOUSE SUMMER
ANGELA'S RETURN HOME
LOVE AMONG THE ARTS
FINN'S FOREST

# MARGARET MOUNSDON

♦

# LOVE IN
# A MIST

*Complete and Unabridged*

## LINFORD
*Leicester*

First published in Great Britain in 2015

First Linford Edition
published 2017

A catalogue record for this book is available
from the British Library.

ISBN 978–1–4448–3149–8

Published by
F. A. Thorpe (Publishing)
Anstey, Leicestershire

Set by Words & Graphics Ltd.
Anstey, Leicestershire
Printed and bound in Great Britain by
T. J. International Ltd., Padstow, Cornwall

This book is printed on acid-free paper

# 1

Fire Alarm was chirping vigorously. Penny envied the bird its stamina. She and Elizabeth had christened the fledgling 'Fire Alarm' when it had perched on the kitchen windowsill for an entire morning and given full throttle to its vocal cords, sounding for all the world like the emergency alarm in Elizabeth's classroom.

Penny sighed. She wished her feathered friend could inject some of its vocal enthusiasm into her figures. Whichever way she studied them, they did not make good reading. She ran her fingers through her blonde hair, causing the wayward strands to frizz up in corkscrew curls.

Customers placed their pets in her care with confidence, and they had a right to expect Penny to keep to her professional part of the deal and not cut corners.

The sound of Elizabeth's laughter floated up from the garden. It gladdened Penny's heart. When her daughter started sleepwalking, Penny realised that living on the top floor of a high-rise block of flats was not an option. It had been a traumatic two years since the loss of her husband Steve; but once they'd taken the plunge and moved from London out into the Kent countryside, life had begun to settle into a routine, and Elizabeth's night-time traumas gradually became a thing of the past.

Penny loved running her own pet-grooming parlour, and business was beginning to take off; but a month earlier, fate had dealt her another life-changing blow, and she knew she had to face up to the possibility that she and Elizabeth were going to have to move again.

Penny frowned as the noise level in the garden increased. She'd left her daughter out planting pansies while she caught up on her paperwork. Elizabeth loved bright colours, and the purple and yellow petals of the pansies were exactly what were needed to brighten up the semi-circular flowerbed the two of them had weeded over the weekend.

Penny glanced at her watch. Alice wasn't due back from dog-walking duties yet, but she could definitely hear barking. She stood on tiptoe and peered out of the window. Tucked away under the eaves, the attic was a perfect choice for somewhere to work undisturbed. It also meant she could keep an eye on the goings-on in the garden.

Down on the lawn, Bracken, the loveliest-natured sheepdog in the world, was exercising his wicked sense of fun by running around the garden and chasing butterflies off the buddleia. Penny's smile faded as she saw to her horror that someone had left the gate open. She dared not call out. Bracken would be off like a flash at the sound of her voice, and the consequences didn't bear thinking about. Not much traffic frequented their lane, but they had experienced the occasional speeding vehicle driven by young men off the neighbouring housing estate.

How Bracken had managed to escape from the day room where he was supposed to be taking his rest, Penny could not imagine. The young salesman had assured her the new lock was dog-proof, but it would seem he was wrong. The Bracken-proof door handle had yet to be invented.

Taking care to make as little noise as possible, Penny crept down the rickety staircase at the side of the old theatre. The treads creaked alarmingly, and along with his other talents Bracken possessed exceptional hearing.

Penny shaded her eyes against the glare of the sun. Elizabeth and Bracken had disappeared. Her daughter knew better than to run into the road, but if she thought Bracken was in trouble she wouldn't hesitate to go to the dog's rescue.

From the direction of the pond there was a loud splash, followed by a shocked squeal. The pond was a homemade affair, constructed with the help of a black dustbin liner and decorated with seashells. It was not deep, but Elizabeth was nervous around water and couldn't swim.

'Elizabeth!' Penny was now past caring who heard her shriek.

Rounding the corner at full speed, she collided with a figure limping towards her. They bounced off each other. Penny staggered back against what had once been the theatre box office; then, recovering her balance, she stared at the man's dishevelled appearance. Pondweed clung to his suit, and his trousers dripped water onto the flagstones.

Bracken bounded over, his tail wagging expectantly. He gave Penny a playful nudge as if inviting her to join in the game.

'I saw it all,' a breathless voice broke into the scenario before Penny could regain her powers of speech. 'Sorry,' Alice gulped, trying to cope with four entangled leads and an overexcited Bracken. 'I stopped to close the gate. Did you leave it open?' She glared at the dripping man.

Before he could reply, Bracken reared up on his hind legs and, catching the visitor off balance, nudged him backwards onto the grass. The small garden was now a scene of absolute mayhem. Five dogs ran round in circles. Alice, unable to cope with their leads, lost her balance and landed on top of the man floundering on the grass. Elizabeth and Penny were reduced to running after their charges in an attempt to restrain them before they caused any more damage, leaving their two hapless victims to sort themselves out. The dogs, sensing another new game, vied with each other to see who could avoid being caught the longest.

'Enough!' Penny bellowed in her best sergeant major's voice. Everyone came to a halt; and, seizing the moment, Penny snatched up the trailing leads. 'Hold these, Elizabeth,' she instructed her daughter, 'while I help Alice.'

'I'm fine,' the teenager said as she struggled to her feet, 'but I don't know about the townie.' She cast a disgusted look at the man who was still struggling to regain his composure, her diamond stud catching the sunlight as she wrinkled her nose. Her gelled spiky hair hadn't moved during the encounter, but the chains on her leather jacket were in need of some attention.

'Who are you?' Penny asked while Alice unhooked the links from her pocket buttons.

'And don't you know the first rule of the countryside? All gates to be closed.' Alice's purple nail varnish flashed in the sunlight as she fiddled with her accessories.

'If I could get to my feet . . . ' The man spoke with a soft Scottish accent.

Penny took pity on his plight. 'You are a mess. Here.' She put out a helping hand.

'I can manage,' was the stiff reply.

'As you wish.' Penny's sympathy

evaporated as he glared at Bracken.

'At the risk of being labelled a tell-tale,' the man said, plucking stray grass cuttings from his sleeve, 'I should look closer to home for the gate-opening culprit.'

Bracken, not in the least intimidated by the expression on his face, smiled back at him and thumped his tail against his legs.

'Would it be too much to ask you to keep your animals under control?'

'Bracken was not out of control. He likes to play,' Penny began to explain.

'He didn't harm you, did he?' Alice asked.

'I'll let you know when my back has fully recovered.'

Penny frowned. 'Have we met before?' There was something vaguely familiar about the visitor.

'I don't think so.'

Bracken chose this moment to give a friendly bark. The man stepped back-wards.

'There's no need to be scared.' Penny

grabbed the dog's collar.

'I was attacked by a Labrador as a child.'

Alice was having none of it. 'Nonsense. They're lovely dogs. You must have upset him. Besides, it may have escaped your attention, but Bracken isn't a Labrador.'

The air crackled between them.

'Why don't we all take a breather and calm down?' Penny smiled at everyone. If Alice took against someone, his or her life wasn't worth living.

Alice ignored Penny's attempts to lighten the mood. 'Where's your sense of humour, you big bully?'

'I find nothing funny about falling into a smelly pond, then being flattened to the ground by a dog with behavioural issues.' The man was now doing his best to repair the damage to his polished shoes.

Penny felt honour-bound to come to Bracken's defence. 'Bracken was only playing.'

'Clearly we have different standards

when it comes to that sort of thing.'

'Lighten up,' Alice said. 'When did you forget to be a human being?'

With a sinking heart, Penny recognised the expression on Alice's face. She was ready to take things further. 'Please, Alice,' she said, increasing her pressure on her arm, 'why don't you take Bracken and the others into the day room? Elizabeth, help Alice. You can groom Bracken. You know how he loves it when you brush him.'

'I want to stay in the garden.' Elizabeth thrust out her jaw, a stubborn expression on her face. At times she looked so like Steve it was difficult for Penny to be strict with her daughter, but today she wasn't prepared to be lenient.

'Please do as you're told,' she forced herself to say in her no-nonsense voice. She rarely used it on her daughter.

Recognising that her mother meant business, Elizabeth shrugged her shoulders and, with a show of injured pride, took two of the leads from Alice.

'Come on,' she mumbled, and dragging her feet across the lawn, made for the day centre. Bracken bounded along beside her, leaving Alice to bring up the rear.

Penny turned back to the unwelcome visitor, who was hopping about on one foot shaking the last of the water out of his shoe. She did her best to retrieve the situation. 'Would you like to freshen up?' He didn't answer. 'You're not going to sue, are you?' The prospect of legal costs to add to her other worries was the last thing Penny needed. 'What happened was an accident, but I'd be pleased to pay any dry-cleaning expenses and buy you a new pair of shoes.' Her face ached from smiling so hard.

'That won't be necessary,' was the clipped reply.

'Then how can I help you?'

'By telling me your name.'

'Penny Graham.'

'And what do you do here?'

'I run a pet-grooming parlour.' She

gestured towards the old theatre complex that housed her work premises and personal accommodation.

'What exactly does that entail?'

'We pamper people's pets for the day.'

'A beauty parlour for dogs?' His voice was full of barely disguised disbelief.

Penny refused to rise to his bait. 'We provide other services too. Bracken's owners are away. They travel a lot and can't take him with them, so he's boarding at the moment. He has special needs.' She didn't think this was the right moment to explain that Bracken had been banned from the local kennels for disruptive behaviour, a legacy of his mistreated past. 'And if you have a dog that needs its nails clipped, then you've come to the right place,' she did her best to finish on a bright note.

'I am not a prospective client.' The tone of the man's voice suggested that this was the last place he would consider for service of any kind.

'Are you an inspector?' Penny was

horror-struck by the thought. She looked around for a briefcase, but there was no sign of any official-looking papers. 'If you are, I can tell you our records are exemplary. All our insurance is up to date, and can be viewed in the office. We follow directives to the letter.'

'I'm pleased to hear it,' the man answered with a wry twist of his lips. 'However, neither is inspecting your records the reason for my visit.'

A cold lump of dread lodged in Penny's chest. The sun caught the distinctive colours of the board at the gate highlighting the words 'For Sale'. 'Are you a solicitor?' she asked. 'You look like one in that suit; or rather, you did before recent events.' Penny always spoke too much when she was nervous, and right now her heart was thumping out a drumbeat that would break all records.

'I am wearing this suit because I have been to visit my solicitors.'

'Do you always talk like that?' Penny enquired.

'Like what?' The man looked nonplussed.

'Sort of stuffy.'

'I'm sorry you find good manners stuffy.'

Penny tried to repair the situation. 'What I meant was . . . '

The man held up a hand to silence her. 'Before you say anything else, perhaps I should introduce myself. My name is Roger Oakes.' He looked at her expectantly.

'Should that mean something to me?' she asked.

'I am Minnie Hyde's grandson.'

Penny looked him up and down. 'You can't be,' she gasped.

'I assure you I am.'

'Then you're . . . ' Penny swallowed, her voice giving out on her.

'The new owner of Cherry Tree Farmhouse,' Roger finished the sentence for her.

# 2

Penny stared at Roger Oakes, taking in every detail of his appearance from his reddish-brown hair to the freckles on his face and his deep blue eyes. Even though he was holding his shoes in his hands, he still towered over her.

'Grandson?' she echoed.

'Yes.'

'I don't believe you.'

'Why should I lie?'

'She never mentioned a grandson to me.'

'Without wishing to appear impolite, the family situation is none of your business.'

'It is when it involves my livelihood.' Penny put a hand to her forehead as if flicking away a tiresome insect. Her thoughts were in a jumble. She had assumed that once the cottage was sold, she would be given a reasonable amount of time to make alternative arrangements. 'You can't evict me.'

'I can't?'

'I have legal rights.'

Roger raised an eyebrow. 'Do you?'

'I could get a holding order.'

'Do you know what that would entail?' He called Penny's bluff by further enquiring, 'Do you even know what you're talking about?'

Restraining the impulse to launch a physical attack on Roger Oakes and start beating him on the chest for destroying her new idyllic life, Penny shook her head. They both realised it had been an empty threat. Penny's business arrangement with Minnie, such as it was, had been very informal. In the beginning there had been talk about a contract to make things official, but neither of them had got round to drawing anything up. Minnie was not hot on paperwork, and Penny had been otherwise engaged with sorting out her own domestic affairs and getting Elizabeth settled into her new life.

Drafting a contract had been the last thing on anyone's mind.

When Penny had first seen Minnie's advert asking for a female companion, she had had no idea that Miss Hyde had been one of the leading actresses of her day. After a stellar career on the stage and a flamboyant personal life, Miss Hyde had settled down to peaceful retirement in a cottage in the Weald countryside. From the moment Penny had first met Minnie, with Elizabeth in tow, the two women had bonded.

'Miss Hyde,' Penny had begun that day, anxious to explain that she had nothing to do with the stage and had only read Minnie's advert in a magazine in the hairdresser's because she was helping out with the shampooing while the regular lady was on holiday.

'Minnie, please,' she had insisted.

'Very well, Minnie.' Penny paused, uncertain how to carry on.

'Darling,' Minnie had gushed, waving

away Penny's further attempts to explain the reason why she was in need of somewhere to live, 'you are my lifesaver.'

'I am?' Penny repeated.

'You would not believe how dreary the other two applicants were — a woman with big teeth and her equally ghastly sister.' Minnie shuddered. 'I don't care if they claimed their father had played Hamlet to my Ophelia, I wasn't having them in my house.'

'What exactly are you looking for?' Penny hoped she wouldn't be asked to recite a Shakespearian soliloquy.

'Company. You are young, you're beautiful, and you've got the most darling little girl. I know we are going to get along famously.'

'I've no experience of this type of thing,' Penny felt duty-bound to volunteer.

'Neither have I,' Minnie responded, 'but I hate being lonely, and I'm of an age where I can no longer give parties. It's funny how so-called friends fade away when they realise there's no more free champagne on offer.'

'Do you think Elizabeth and I would fit in?' Penny stroked her daughter's hair. The child hadn't uttered a word since they had arrived. Penny prayed Elizabeth wouldn't take against Minnie. The dress the actress was wearing was a bit weird. Penny wondered if it was a Shakespeare heroine's cast-off. It certainly looked glamorous enough for grand theatre. Elizabeth was staring at it and Minnie as if entranced.

'I've no doubt about it at all, darling.' Minnie put a hand to her chest as a look of apprehension crossed her face. 'You wouldn't mind,' she continued, fiddling with her necklace, 'if I'm the teeniest bit eccentric on occasions, would you?'

Penny blinked. 'In what way?' she asked in a careful voice.

'I tend to wander around the garden at any time, day or night. It's my roses, you see. They need attention, and sometimes I forget I'm wearing my nightdress. The neighbours complain. Well, one neighbour in particular, actually.'

Elizabeth spoke for the first time. 'I like flowers,' she said. 'Roses are pretty and they smell nice.'

Minnie beamed at the child. 'There, it's all settled. You can have the flat over the theatre so we won't get in each other's way. This is going to be such fun.'

'Theatre?'

'David, my third husband, and I built it after we moved down here. We ran an acting school.' Minnie's violet eyes lost some of their sparkle. 'I was heartbroken when we had to close it down. The bank manager refused to extend our loan. Can you believe it? Businessmen do not appreciate the arts. All they see are figures for their wretched balance sheets.'

'I'm sorry,' was all Penny could think of to say.

Minnie shrugged off her melancholy. 'Well, no use crying over spilt milk.

Back to the matter in hand. When can you move in?'

It was only later, when Penny looked her up online, that she realised the extent of Minnie's fame. Statuesque, flame-haired and outstandingly beautiful, Penny read how the moment Minnie stepped onto the stage it came to life. Using her classically trained husky voice to full effect, she became the character she was playing; and the audiences, stirred by the emotions she created, wept and laughed with her. There wasn't a male in the audience who didn't long to protect her, and the women wanted to share her anguish and her pain.

Minnie's private life had been as colourful as her acting career. Widowed three times, each of her marriages had been to members of the profession, and each marriage had been a clash of egos and a battle of wills. Penny had learned that Minnie's constant extravagances had more than once brought her to the brink of bankruptcy.

Cherry Tree Farmhouse was as beautiful as its name suggested. It had originally been part of a working farm, but over the years the land had been sold off to fund Minnie's theatre and pay off other outstanding debts.

'One has to make sacrifices for one's art,' she explained to Penny, 'but you'll never know how much it cost me to give up my theatre school.'

Sensing there might be more to her story than Minnie was prepared to reveal, Penny had not enquired further. Instead they made plans for Penny and Elizabeth to move in.

The three of them had enjoyed eighteen happy months together. In winter they would settle down in front of roaring log fires while Minnie entertained them with stories about her time in the theatre. Then as the days lengthened into summer, they would work in the garden of an evening, tending to Minnie's beloved roses.

'Just a little longer, darling,' Minnie

would beg as it became too dark to see what they were doing. Occasionally, to her consternation, Penny would catch sight of Minnie in the garden at dawn; and on another occasion after an extremely dry spell, she saw her watering her garden at midnight. It was after one such foray that Minnie caught a severe chill that went straight to her chest.

Penny dragged her thoughts back to the present and tried to focus on Roger Oakes. It was no good dwelling on the past. 'What plans do you have for the cottage?' she asked him.

'I intend to sell up, but first I need to sort out my grandmother's affairs. I believe she had an ongoing feud with one of her neighbours — something to do with property boundaries?'

'Lydia Gerald?' Penny's shoulders sagged.

Lydia too had been an actress, using the stage name of Desmonde Vale. When she had married the renowned contemporary artist Liam Phoenix, she had cut down on her career commitments for a life of domesticity. With Liam's rise in his fortunes, they were able to bid for Minnie's land as it went under the hammer each time Minnie found herself in distressed financial circumstances. The two ladies indulged in frequent spats over the exact amount of land Lydia now owned. All Penny knew of the feud was that Lydia had plans to sell off the land her late husband had purchased to the highest bidder.

'My solicitor tells me they have already started talks with Ms Gerald.'

Penny straightened her shoulders. There was nothing she could do about the situation. It was best to accept the inevitable and leave with her dignity intact. 'When do you want me to move out?'

'There's no hurry.' Roger held up his hands in a gesture of conciliation.

'I thought you were giving me notice to quit.'

'There are a lot of legal hoops to

jump through first.'

Neither of them had heard Alice come round the corner from the day room. 'Leave?' Her shrill voice fractured the air. 'You can't throw Penny out. You can't.' She was breathing heavily, her pale skin highlighted by two bright red splodges of colour on her cheeks.

'Nothing's been decided, Alice,' Penny stepped in before Roger could reply. 'Mr Oakes and I were discussing the situation, that's all.'

'I heard him say — ' Alice struggled to catch her breath. ' — that you had to leave.'

'I said no such thing,' Roger protested.

With calm efficiency, Penny squashed Roger's toes with the heel of her sandals. He bit down an oath and shot her a look of anguish. 'Sorry,' Penny said, smiling sweetly, 'was that your foot?'

'You know it was,' he gasped through gritted teeth.

Penny turned away from him. 'Why don't you take the rest of the day off, Alice? I'm sure your father could do with some help.'

'What did you do that for?' Roger hissed as a disconsolate Alice closed the garden gate behind her.

'Alice suffers from stress-related agoraphobia. It can bring on breathing difficulties. I didn't want her having an attack.'

Roger looked round, a puzzled frown creasing his brow. 'How can she walk dogs if she's agoraphobic?'

'It's part of her relief therapy.' Penny waved away his further questions. 'Can we please make another appointment if you intend to discuss our ongoing issues? There are things I really need to do. The senior citizens' bus is due tomorrow afternoon, and I have to be prepared for the unexpected.'

'Surely you don't expect senior citizens to run amok?' Roger half laughed in disbelief.

'The pat-a-dog scheme,' Penny explained.

'Everyone loves their afternoon tea, too. I have to order extra supplies.'

'I didn't realise you had such a commitment to the community.'

'It was Minnie's idea and I'm totally on side with it. She used to love entertaining everyone with poetry readings and tales of the stage.'

'I'm sorry I never heard her perform. Everyone tells me she was young at heart.'

For a second Penny felt sorry for Roger, until she remembered the reason why Minnie had advertised for a live-in companion. She had been lonely. Surely the occasional visit from her grandson wouldn't have caused him too much hardship? 'Where are you staying?' Penny asked him.

'I've booked a room at The King's Head.'

A dimple dented Penny's cheek as she tried not to laugh.

'What's so funny?' Roger asked.

'You could be in for an interesting stay. Len Humphries is the landlord.'

'I've met him.'

'What do you think of him?'

'He's a man who doesn't mince his words.'

'He's also Alice's father,' Penny added, and watched the colour drain from Roger's face.

'I didn't realise.'

'It doesn't do to rub him up the wrong way, and I'm sure Alice will have updated him on all this afternoon's activities.'

Roger struggled back into his shoes, grimacing as his feet squelched inside their socks. 'I suppose I'd better go and face the music. I'm sorry about your gate. I know I closed it behind me.'

'The catch is loose,' Penny admitted. 'John was supposed to have fixed it, but like a lot of others things he never got round to it.

'Is John your husband?'

'No. He's the handyman.'

'And you live here alone with your daughter?'

'I'm a single mother. I was your

28

grandmother's companion for eighteen months.'

'I see.' Roger glanced down at Penny's left hand.

'Although I'm widowed,' she said, 'I still wear my wedding ring.' She wiggled her fingers at him.

'I didn't mean to be nosey,' Roger apologised.

'As we're into family circumstances, I have to say that until today I didn't know of your existence.'

'I was born in Scotland,' Roger explained.

'A world away,' Penny agreed.

Roger looked as though he were about to say something more, but before he could speak a voice interrupted them. 'I've finished grooming Bracken.' Elizabeth was now standing beside her mother. 'Are you staying on for dinner?' she asked Roger. 'We've got egg and chips. I collected the eggs this morning. They were all golden-brown and warm.'

'Mr Oakes is a busy man, darling,'

Penny said. 'He doesn't have time to eat egg and chips.'

'We've got brown bread soldiers too,' Elizabeth coaxed. 'I buttered them myself.'

'Another time.' The lines around Roger's eyes creased into a smile, softening the expression in his blue eyes. 'Brown bread soldiers are the best.'

He and Elizabeth exchanged happy looks. Roger then looked expectantly at Penny. 'Maybe we could meet up tomorrow night for a meal at The King's Head?'

Elizabeth clapped her hands excitedly. 'Afterwards I could play that new computer game with Alice. She's promised to show me how to beat the girls in my class. I never win,' she confided to Roger.

'I'm not sure,' Penny said.

In the distance they heard the unmistakeable sound of a dog barking. 'It's Bracken,' Elizabeth giggled. 'I suspect he's undone the day-room latch again.' A look of unease crossed Roger's face.

'Perhaps you'd better leave,' Penny advised, 'and please make sure this time you close the gate firmly behind you.'

'Tomorrow night, seven o'clock?' Roger called back as he hastened down the drive.

'I like Mr Oakes,' Elizabeth said, 'don't you, Mummy?'

With a sad smile, Penny followed her daughter into their flat. Whether she liked him or not, Roger Oakes was the enemy. He had the power to change their lives and he was about to exercise his rights.

# 3

Tuneless whistling stirred Penny from an unsatisfactory night's sleep. After tossing and turning until dawn, she eventually dozed off as the first of the sun's rays began to colour the horizon orange and Fire Alarm had performed a few experimental tweets.

'Mummy.' Elizabeth shook her shoulder. 'John's here. I've been dressed for hours. Can I go and look for eggs? And can we have porridge for breakfast? I'm very hungry.'

Penny struggled with the bedclothes and eventually blinked herself awake.

'Your hair's standing on end.' Elizabeth giggled. 'It makes you look like a leprechaun.'

'Tell John I'll be down in a minute.' Penny scrambled out of bed. 'And be careful not to tread on any stray eggs.'

'I won't,' Elizabeth's voice floated

back at her as she jumped down the stairs and out into the garden.

'Steady on, Princess,' John called after her. 'What's the hurry?'

'Busy,' she replied.

He laughed as Elizabeth raced past him towards the hencoop. He tested the latch he was mending, then tightened the screw before securing the gate.

'I don't know how long this one will hold once Bracken gets his paws on it,' he explained to Penny as she and Bracken strolled down the path to greet him, 'but I've done my best. You're a very naughty boy, aren't you?' Bracken licked his hand.

'Thanks, John. Fancy a coffee?' Penny offered.

'Thought you'd never ask.' He threw his tools into his box, then depositing it in the log store, followed Penny up to the first floor kitchen.

'So what's this rumour buzzing round the village about Minnie's grandson?' he asked, taking a biscuit out of the tin.

Bracken lapped up some water, then settled down in a sunny corner. Resting his head on his paws, he began to snore.

Penny stirred the porridge. 'Have you met Roger Oakes?'

'No, but Len's full of it. He's Minnie's long-lost grandson, is that right?'

'So he claims.'

'Hm.' John chewed on another biscuit, then stirred two spoonfuls of sugar into his coffee. 'How come no one's ever heard of him?'

'He said it was because he lived in Scotland.'

'Want me to find out more?' John asked. 'My contacts stretch far and wide.'

'No need. We're having dinner together tonight.'

'Are you indeed?' John arched an eyebrow. 'Have I reason to be concerned?'

Penny cast him an impatient look. She couldn't count the number of times she had told him she liked him but only as a friend. He had something of a reputation locally, and she had no wish to be another of his conquests. Steve had been the only man for her, and whilst she had been on a few dates over the past year, they had amounted to nothing serious. These days her life was her work and Elizabeth, and now it would seem finding somewhere new to live.

'There are things Roger and I need to discuss, and yesterday wasn't convenient,' she explained.

'I heard about the shenanigans with Bracken. Pity he didn't finish the job with Roger.' He added when Penny looked confused, 'You should have scared him off for once and for all, my Bracken, shouldn't you?' He stroked the sleepy dog's fur. Bracken's tail thumped the floor and he made a satisfied noise at the back of his throat.

'Like it or not,' Penny said, 'Roger has plans for Cherry Tree Farmhouse.'

'Poor old Minnie,' John commiserated. 'She would have been so upset to learn you were being evicted.'

'Minnie was nothing if not practical,' Penny pointed out. 'I don't think she would have thought much of me if I'd not faced up to the challenge full on. 'Live for the day' was her mantra, and that's what I intend to do. I always knew I couldn't stay on forever.'

John didn't look convinced. 'All the same, it doesn't seem fair.'

'There's nothing we can do about it. Anyway, for the moment life goes on as normal.'

'I could make things difficult,' John suggested. 'The farmhouse chimney's wobbly, and I could distress a few loose tiles on the roof.'

'How would that help?'

John sighed. 'I don't know, really. It might reduce Roger's enthusiasm to sell, and it might give you more time.'

'The farmhouse is a character property. People expect crooked chimneys. Besides, I'd rather you didn't interfere.

I can deal with this on my own.'

'Anything you say.'

'Elizabeth,' Penny called out the window, 'breakfast's ready.'

'If there's any of that porridge going spare,' John said, grabbing another bowl, 'I could use some.'

'You've eaten four biscuits.'

'It's hungry work, mending things.'

Penny watched the steam rise from the three healthy portions she served up. John could be infuriating, and he wasn't the most reliable of individuals, but Penny counted him as a friend, and she doubted there would be many more intimate breakfasts such as these.

John finished off his breakfast with two slices of toast. 'Have you spoken to Lydia?'

'I'm amazed she hasn't been round,' Penny admitted as she collected up the plates. 'She's always poking her head over the hedge on the slightest excuse, and there was enough disturbance yesterday to wake an army.'

'You've got to make allowances,' John

said with a surprising show of generosity. 'She's lonely now she can't bicker with Minnie anymore. It's natural she should take an interest in what everyone else is up to.'

'Anybody in?' a voice called up the stairs.

'Talk of angels.' John pushed back his chair. 'I'll be off. If you need me, I'll be working at Marika's Moderns all day. Mind if I nip out the back way?' He disappeared down the rear stairs.

Lydia poked her head round the kitchen door. 'Did I hear voices?' She eyed up the remains of their breakfast.

'John's been fixing the gate,' Penny explained, adding, 'He couldn't stay. He's got a busy day.'

'Obviously he's too busy with the glamorous Marika Wilczeski to finish off my patio. He really is the limit. If there's any coffee left, I wouldn't say no. Black, no sugar.'

Penny sighed. Why was it no one seemed to realise she had a business to run and that she was not here at everyone's beck and call?

'Can I get down now please?' Elizabeth asked. 'I've finished my egg.'

'Off you go, darling, but remember — no running into the lane. John's mended the gate, so there's no need for you to touch it.'

'I want to weed my flowerbed.' Elizabeth struggled into her flowered boots. 'And my teacher says she'll give me some love in a mist seeds to sow. The flowers are all pretty and blue.'

'No school today?' Lydia enquired.

'It's a teachers' seminar.' Elizabeth stomped on the floor as her heel stuck in the back of her boot. Penny realised to her dismay that her daughter was already outgrowing the last present she had received from Minnie.

Lydia waved away the biscuits. 'I dropped by because I have some news for you.' Her grey eyes were alight with excitement. 'I've had an approach from the solicitors dealing with Minnie's estate. They want to know if I'm still interested in selling my part of the land.'

'They haven't wasted much time.' Penny sat down opposite Lydia and bit into a shortbread finger.

'Perhaps I will treat myself, just this once.' Lydia followed Penny's example and took a plain biscuit off the plate. Despite her age, she was still enviably slim, and regular pilates classes ensured she kept her trim figure.

'Will you put in an offer for the rest of the property?' Penny asked.

'There are complications.' Lydia paused for theatrical effect. 'It would seem Minnie didn't leave a will.'

'That shouldn't present too much of a problem, should it?' Penny asked.

'I understand from my daily that Minnie's grandson was here yesterday.' Lydia took another biscuit and nibbled on it with an absent-minded frown.

'He came to introduce himself.'

'I'm sorry I missed him. I had a wretched committee meeting, otherwise I would have been here,' Lydia explained. 'Anyway, the authorities have to do searches and go through various processes to make sure there are no other interested parties, all of which takes time.'

'Did you know Minnie had family?' Penny asked, upset at the thought of strangers claiming on her estate.

'Liam and I only moved down here when Minnie was married to her last husband, David. She was so involved in her theatre workshops that having a child would have been the last thing on her mind, I should imagine — though I do vaguely remember Liam saying something about a child by her second husband.' Lydia finished her biscuit. 'Of course, Minnie was older than me, so there are gaps in her life I know nothing about. It wasn't unknown for actresses to separate their private lives from their professional lives. Children have a habit of growing up, and it's no good pretending you're twenty-one when your daughter is sixteen, if you get my drift.'

Penny hid a smile. Lydia liked to give the impression there was a significant age gap between herself and Minnie.

'Minnie was scatterbrained and a law unto herself, so I'm not surprised her affairs are in a mess. That was why Liam and I helped her out by buying her land when she needed funds.'

Penny remembered Minnie confessing to her one day: 'Liam Phoenix was quite a man — very attractive, with masses of dark hair, lots of brooding masculinity. I was never interested in him, but that didn't stop him from paying a visit whenever the mood was on him. I don't think Lydia ever quite believed me when I said there was nothing between us.' A wicked twinkle sparkled in Minnie's eyes at the memory. 'I may have been guilty of slightly misleading her.'

'Minnie,' Penny chided.

'Well she would keep making insinuations about my Portia. Said I was too old for the part. She lost out to me, you see. The director cast me in the lead and Lydia never forgave either of us.'

Penny shook her head. It was her secret belief that Lydia had been as distraught as Penny when Minnie had passed away, but for appearances' sake she had kept up the pretence of their feud.

'Did Roger suggest you would need to start looking round for new premises?' Lydia asked. 'I mean, I wouldn't want to evict you, Penny — you know that; I'm not even sure I have the right to. But ... ' She shrugged her shoulders. ' ... half of this land is already mine, and whilst I never pursued the matter with Minnie, I think I need to get the situation sorted out before some scoundrel lays false claim to the property. I'm not suggesting this Roger Oakes isn't who he says he is, but with Minnie you never knew where you were. She could have long-lost relatives all over the world for all we know.'

Penny had to acknowledge the truth of Lydia's words. Of an evening Minnie would regale her with stories of her fellow actors, but Penny had difficulty remembering their names, and in the great tradition of the theatre many of the people who were mentioned had been married to each other, often more than once.

'Anyway,' Lydia said as she finished her coffee, 'must dash. I've a hairdressing appointment.'

★   ★   ★

'All set?' John Warren nudged open the door to Marika's Moderns with his foot, put down his toolbox, and smiled at the tall, dark-haired woman at the desk. 'Hello?' he repeated his greeting when he didn't get an immediate response. 'Anyone home?'

Marika looked up from the letter she had been studying, her dark brown eyes full of confusion. 'I don't understand,' she said.

'What's the matter?' John was at her side in an instant.

Marika's English was fluent, but

occasionally her knowledge of the language was put to the test, especially when she was stressed. 'It says here notice to vacate.'

'What?' John snatched the letter from her grasp and ran his eye down the typewritten page. 'Looks like your landlord's giving you the boot,' he said as he finished reading.

'The boot?' Marika frowned.

'You're going to have to find somewhere new to live.'

'But I have paid six months' rent in advance. Why should I move?'

'Asbestos. It's poisonous stuff. Your landlord's had a survey done and they've found evidence of it in the roof. You can't stay on.'

'Why?'

'Why what?' John handed back the letter.

'I have to leave?' Marika tucked a stray lock of hair behind her ear in a gesture of bewilderment.

'Why don't I make us a nice cup of tea?' John suggested, turning the sign on the door to 'closed' and clicking the latch down.

'Wednesday is one of my busiest days,' Marika protested.

'We need to talk, and you're not in the mood for customers today.'

The range of fashion on offer in Marika's boutique provided a broad choice, from edgy and contemporary to classic chic. Marika Wilczeski, an ex-model, had taken over the running of the shop after the previous owner had retired. She knew how fashion worked and how to get things done. John had helped her with the refurbishment, and they were now on the last stage of finishing off the changing rooms.

'The bank they lend me money, but I have reached my limit. I am maxed out.'

'Here you are.' John plonked a mug of tea onto the table in front of Marika. 'Hot, strong and sweet, just the thing for shock. Get that down you.'

Marika sipped the scalding liquid. They were sitting in the tiny kitchen at the back of the shop. John had opened the door, and a brave ray of sunshine was doing its best to warm things up.

'I have no money to find new premises.'

'Different landlord. Everything's fine with the shop,' John assured her. 'No need to worry there.'

'You think?' Marika didn't look convinced. 'It is difficult to find somewhere new to live. When I first came to this country, I lived in a hostel, but I had to leave after six months. I cannot go back there. It is not what I have been used to. What am I going to do? Everywhere is so expensive. All my money has been invested in the shop. I cannot now afford to pay your bill. You must go.' She made a shooing gesture at him.

'Don't worry about that, and I'm staying put.' John squeezed Marika's hand. 'We'll sort something out about the bill later. Right now it's more important to find somewhere for you to live.'

'The letter says with immediate effect. This asbestos it is dangerous? Perhaps I can persuade the landlord to let me stay?'

'You'll do no such thing.' John was firm on that score. 'Asbestos poses a serious health hazard. I suppose you couldn't use the premises over the shop?'

'The flat is occupied, and it would be far too expensive for me to rent anyway.'

'Hm.' John screwed up his face in thought. 'For the moment you could stay at The King's Head. I'm sure Len will do you a special rate if I mention your circumstances.' He flapped the enclosed cheque at her. 'At least your landlord was decent enough to refund you the full amount of your deposit cheque.'

'I will have to close the shop.'

'No you won't,' John assured her. 'Don't keep interrupting; I'm beginning to get an idea.'

'You are?' Marika took another

experimental sip of her tea. It was too sweet for her taste but it was warming her up. She smiled at John. Her years on the catwalk had taught her that men often responded to her smile. It was another way to get things done, and she was in desperate need of help.

'How do you fancy staying in a seventeenth-century farmhouse cottage?'

'What are you talking about? Where is this cottage?'

'In the country near the new housing estate. It's a bit of a walk from the bus stop, but there's a regular service. It would do you good to get out into the country; you're far too pale and you look tired. You're in need of some good fresh air in your lungs, and there's plenty of that in St Mary's.'

The dark circles under Marika's eyes were evidence that she hadn't been sleeping well. 'I am a city girl. At home I live in the middle of the student area. It is buzzing. There is life. I don't want to be a vegetable in this St Mary's.'

John grinned. Marika was a spirited woman, and he was glad to see she was getting her spark back. 'You won't be a vegetable. I'll be round to see you every day. I'm always visiting Penny Graham. She's a lovely lady. She lives above the converted theatre with her daughter and runs a pets' parlour. Then there's that retired actress, Lydia Gerald — Desmonde Vale?'

Marika looked perplexed. 'Who?'

'She'd be your new neighbour. You must remember her; she's our local celebrity. Didn't she attend your open day? She made a speech. Wore a gold lamé dress covered in sequins, and painted her fingernails to match.'

Marika's eyes widened. 'Lydia Gerald lives next door to Cherry Tree Farmhouse, doesn't she?'

'That's right.'

'I could not live there.'

'Why not?'

'It's up for sale.'

'It's empty at the moment.'

'I cannot squat.'

'I'm not suggesting you do anything illegal.'

'Then, John, what do you suggest?'

'That you live there until you can make alternative arrangements. If we approached the solicitors, I don't suppose they'd ask very much in the way of rent.'

'How do you know this?'

'Inside knowledge.' John tapped the side of his nose. 'There's been a delay in administering the estate, so it can't be sold until the legalities have been sorted out. The property is in need of renovation, and with it being unoccupied its condition will start to deteriorate.'

Marika shivered. 'I do not like to get involved with authorities.'

'You won't.'

'They say things they don't mean.'

'You leave the authorities to me. Go home and start packing. I'll have a word with my personal contact, then I'll come back and drive you to The King's Head. By the way,' he added, 'I suggest you be nice to Roger Oakes.'

'Who?'

'He owns the farmhouse, and for the time being he's staying at The King's Head. Make sure you bump into him and turn on the charm.'

# 4

Penny spent the rest of the morning trying to finish off the paperwork she had been working on the previous day before Roger's arrival had interrupted her. The telephone rang constantly with people anxious to know if the stories were true that she was moving out or selling up. Word had quickly spread round the village, and the rumour mill had gone into overdrive. Penny, anxious to ensure her clients did not suffer from lack of confidence, did her best to reassure her regulars that for the moment it was business as usual.

The usual influx of dogs after lunch tied up most of her afternoon. Alice took the more excitable ones for a long walk while Penny and her two assistants attended to the dematting, clipping and brushing requirements of those booked in for more personal grooming. It was the part of her job that Penny enjoyed the most, especially the playtime, siesta, and cuddles hour after all their needs had been attended to. There had never been a pet she didn't love.

Bracken was on his best behaviour all day and hadn't attempted to undo John's handiwork on the garden gate. Because of his rescue dog history, Penny suspected that Bracken, a victim of mistreatment, had tried to escape from his owners, and it had remained a character trait he was unable to shake off.

Penny's pat-a-dog scheme was a great success with young and old alike, and the usual party of senior citizens dropped by after partaking of Len's special lunch. 'Really give a sense of community, these afternoons,' one of their number told Penny as she cast an indulgent eye on the antics of two adolescent spaniels chasing their tails. 'I've always had dogs, but they aren't allowed where I am now. I can understand why, but I do miss having a pet to talk to of an evening.'

Alice stood by Penny's side to wave their visitors off. 'Dad and I have been talking about forming a protest group,' she said.

Penny frowned. 'Surely Cherry Tree Farmhouse constitutes a private sale. Hardly worthy of a protest group.'

Alice took in Penny's confused expression. 'Haven't you heard?'

'Heard what?'

'Property developers want to build executive houses on the land.'

'That's an old rumour.'

'If they do, it'll rip the heart out of the village. We can't let that happen, Penny.'

'Lydia says that things have stalled while the legal people do searches. It may all come to nothing.' Alice didn't look convinced.

Penny began clearing away as the owners arrived to collect their pets, and for the next half hour she was too busy to think about anything other than dealing with enquiries, making new appointments, and following up her policy of saying a personal goodbye to every one of the pets booked in for that day.

It all took time, and when she locked up the day room she was running late for her dinner appointment with Roger. At the back of her mind lurked the suspicion that Len might try to persuade her to be the village spokesperson for his proposed action group. As their taxi drove into The King's Head car park, she hoped she was wrong.

'Alice!' Elizabeth jigged up and down in excitement as her friend descended the stairs of The King's Head to greet them.

'Roger's in the lounge waiting for you, Penny,' Alice said. 'Dad's made sure you won't be disturbed. Don't let Mr Oakes upset you. Remember, we're still talking action groups.'

'You don't mind having Elizabeth for the evening?' Penny was reluctant to take advantage of Alice's good nature.

'Dad's made us a plate of brown-bread banana sandwiches, and I've got two DVDs we can watch and a new computer game to play.'

'Wicked. Mummy's given us some chocolates.' Elizabeth produced the sparkly box. 'I like the green ones.'

Alice cast a look over Penny's shoulder. 'You haven't brought Bracken with you? Dad doesn't allow dogs on the premises, only in the garden.'

'His owners collected him this evening,' Penny told her. 'They came back a day early.'

'In that case, power to the people.' Alice did a high-fisted salute. Elizabeth immediately followed her example. Penny smiled, not sure what cause they were championing, but pleased that the pale-faced girl who had virtually had to be dragged to her door about six months ago, her fear of open spaces being so bad, was now acting like a normal teenager, full of angst and ready to change the world.

'Mummy, can I have a nose stud like

Alice's?' Elizabeth asked.

'Not until you're older, and then only if I say so,' Penny replied, hoping Alice would outgrow her Goth phase before Elizabeth became difficult about body piercing.

Alice held out her hand to Elizabeth. 'You're doing rebellion too early. Come on, Princess, we'd best do as Mummy says and behave ourselves.'

'John calls me Princess,' Elizabeth said as she laboured up the steep stairs behind Alice.

'That's because you're special. All princesses are special.'

Still smiling, Penny walked into the lounge. Roger Oakes stood up to greet her. 'Can I get you a drink?' he asked her.

The casual shirt and chinos he was wearing looked less intimidating than his business suit, and Penny did her best to relax. For her part, she had chosen her outfit with care. She didn't want Roger thinking he was dealing with a country bumpkin who spent her life chasing recalcitrant dogs through rose gardens, though why she should care what he thought about her she wasn't sure.

She had complemented her black tank top with a pair of lime-green cargo pants that she'd seen in the window of Marika's Moderns, and had finished off the outfit with the silver pendant that had been Steve's engagement present. She fingered it now. Its smooth touch gave her confidence.

'I'd like a white wine spritzer, please.' She straightened her shoulders in preparation for what was going to be a stimulating encounter.

Len appeared with a glass on a tray. 'I've already poured one out for you, Penny. Nice and cool and dry, exactly how you like it, and a few nibbles to keep you going.' He produced two menus. 'The bar's not busy, but you can eat in here if you prefer.'

Not wanting to be the subject of gossip, Penny agreed to Len's suggestion, and after they'd ordered she leaned back in her chair. 'I'm not sure where to start.'

'Then let me,' Roger said. 'If it's all right with you, I'd prefer to forget about yesterday and start again.' He looked questioningly at her.

Penny nodded agreement. 'I'm prepared to go along with that.'

'I'm not sure exactly how much you know about Minnie's estate.'

'She didn't leave a will, and you may not be the only claimant,' Penny said. 'A search has gone out for other possible beneficiaries.'

Roger acknowledged her words with a smile. 'I'm impressed by the efficiency of St Mary's network.'

'Second to none,' Penny agreed.

He swallowed some of his beer. 'Have you also heard of Marika Wilczeski?'

'I have.' Penny wondered where this line of questioning was going.

'Can you tell me anything about her?'

'She's Polish. I think she comes from Cracow. She has a dress boutique in town; I've been in a couple of times.

That's about it, really. Why?'

'How would you feel about having her as a neighbour?'

'I don't think a dress shop would be compatible with the requirements of a pet-grooming parlour.'

'That's not what I meant.'

'I'm sorry, but I haven't had a chance to look round for alternative premises yet,' Penny cut Roger's explanation short. 'Your arrival yesterday was rather sudden, and if you want me to fall in with any plans you've made on my behalf, then you're out of luck. So the answer to your question is, I would not consider moving in with Marika. The idea's preposterous.'

Roger chewed on a handful of peanuts thoughtfully. 'I agree that the idea of Bracken in a dress shop is enough to give anyone nightmares, and I wasn't for one moment suggesting it.'

'Then what are we talking about?' Penny asked.

'Here we are — two salmon specials with freshly prepared local vegetables.

Don't let it get cold.' Len glared at Roger as he put their meals down on the table.

'I don't think mine host likes me very much.' Roger offered Penny the peppermill.

'Can you blame him? Minnie was popular in the village. None of us realised she had family, and then out of the blue you roll up and announce you're her grandson and that you've inherited her cottage.'

'Actually, we were in touch.' Roger began to eat his salmon.

'You didn't visit very often.'

'Minnie always remembered my birthday and Christmas. I don't think my grandfather on my father's side approved of her giddy ways, and that's why she never came up to Scotland.'

'I'm sorry,' Penny apologised. 'I didn't mean to pry. Your private life is none of my business. What were we talking about?'

'The legal searches are going to take longer than the solicitors envisaged. As you know, Minnie had three husbands, and there are procedures that have to be followed. So for the time being, if you would like to stay on at the theatre, I have no objection.'

Penny felt a weight lift off her shoulders. 'That *is* good news,' she said. 'But I still don't understand why you were asking about Marika.'

'She's interested in lodging in Cherry Tree Farmhouse. There's plenty of space, and I don't like the idea of it being unoccupied.'

'Doesn't Marika rent rooms?'

'She's been given notice to quit.'

'Why don't *you* move into the farmhouse?'

'I travel a lot, so it would suit my plans better if I kept a room on here. If you want to discuss things with Marika, she is staying here for a few days.' Roger finished his salmon and put down his knife and fork. 'In fact, here she is.'

'Darling.' Marika was all smiles as she crossed the room looking stunning in a long peacock-blue dress decorated with bright yellow swirls. Her dark hair was piled high on her head, and she looked every inch the supermodel. She kissed Roger on the cheek and hugged him. 'Hello, Penny.' She turned a triumphant look in Penny's direction. 'I do hope you won't object to Roger's little plan for me. It would be too tiresome if you were to create problems.' Without waiting for Penny's reply, she turned back to Roger. 'You have eaten?' She leaned forward and helped herself to a broccoli floret. 'Such a shame. I am hungry. If I'd known there was salmon on the menu, I would have joined you.'

Roger held out a chair for her. 'Please, sit down. I'm sure Len can come up with something. I'll see what I can arrange.'

Marika waited until he had gone in search of Len before speaking again. 'I hope your dogs won't bark all night and keep me awake. I have early starts in the morning.'

Penny took a deep breath, the

temptation to get her own back on the woman getting the better of her. 'You needn't worry, Marika. I'll be moving on as soon as I can. Then you can have the place to yourself — apart from Charles, that is.'

'Who is Charles?' Marika asked, a note of nervousness in her voice.

'Minnie used to come across to the theatre to sleep if he was being extra difficult. The story goes Charles took refuge in the farmhouse during the civil war and he's never really left. In true cavalier style, he's got an eye for the ladies. I would offer you Minnie's bed in the theatre, as he can at times prove tiresome, but as you don't like dogs you'd best stay in the farmhouse. I shouldn't worry, though — Charles is quite well behaved most of the time. Now I really must be going. I, too, have early starts in the morning. Say goodbye to Roger for me.'

Doing her best not to laugh, Penny left the room and headed upstairs to Alice's bed-sit to collect Elizabeth. The story about the romantic cavalier was one Minnie kept to entertain visitors who asked if the premises were haunted. In truth, the real Charles had been Minnie's nickname for her ancient temperamental boiler, and when it played up Minnie would join Penny and Elizabeth in the theatre 'until the old boy settles down', Minnie would explain.

Penny suspected that the real reason for Minnie's reluctance to spend the night in the farmhouse was because she found the cottage inhospitable when the wind howled down the chimney on stormy nights, but they both kept up the pretence of a misbehaving boiler for appearances' sake.

Penny felt a twinge of remorse as she pushed open Alice's bedroom door. She'd collect Elizabeth, then go back downstairs and apologise to Marika for spinning her a ridiculous tale about ghostly cavaliers.

'Mr Oakes has taken Miss Wilcezski out for something to eat. I've finished serving,' Len explained when Penny found the lounge deserted. 'Want me to pass on a message?'

Penny shook her head. 'I'll catch up with her later,' she replied. If Marika wanted to move into the farmhouse, then making friends with Roger was probably a sensible course of action, she decided.

'Has Alice mentioned anything about a protest group?' Len asked in a quiet voice.

Penny hoped her smile didn't slip. Len could be touchy, and she didn't want to fall out with him. 'Can we await developments?' she asked.

'Don't leave it too long,' Len warned her as he cleared up the last of the glasses from the table. He glanced out of the window. 'Your taxi's here.'

With a sigh, Penny let herself out. How could she have ever thought life in the countryside would be peaceful?

# 5

'You will take care over Lucetta's paws, won't you?' Lydia stroked her pampered Shih Tzu. 'I'm sure last time she got an infection when your clippers nicked her flesh.'

'Don't worry, Lydia,' Penny assured her, 'Lucetta will be fine with us.' She knew there was no such thing as a badly behaved animal, only badly behaved owners, but it was something of a struggle to find something good about Lucetta. Disasters always seemed to happen when she was around. Leads became entangled, grooming equipment mysteriously went astray, and open bottles of shampoo were overturned.

Lydia tweaked the pink bow in Lucetta's hair. 'Did you know I named her after Lucetta, my waiting woman? I played Julia, beloved of Proteus — *Two*

*Gentlemen of Verona.*'

Penny had heard most of Lydia's stories before, and as this morning was proving more than usually hectic, she was only half-listening. 'Is that so?' she answered with one eye on the clock.

'Yes. Well, I'll be back by four. My agent begged me to do a voiceover as a special favour. The regular 'voice' has a throat infection — so unprofessional. In my day we were more careful about what we ate and drank and with whom we mixed before an important booking.'

'I'm sure you were,' Penny replied. It was half past eight in the morning, her busiest time of day, and she really didn't need Lydia Gerald getting in the way.

'Anyway, must be off. They're sending a car and driver for me. They only do that for their stars, but it is a luxury I enjoy. Take care of my little angel. She is so delicate and does require extra attention. Don't hesitate to call if you have any problems, and remember to use my professional name Desmonde

Vale. Best ask for Miss Vale.' Lydia gave a smile of false modesty. 'Protocol must be observed in professional circumstances.'

'Is Elizabeth ready?' The harassed mother doing that week's car pool poked her head round the door, colliding with Lydia. 'Sorry.' Lydia swept past her.

Elizabeth ran through from the kitchen. 'Here I am. Where's my recorder?'

Penny raised her eyebrows. 'You were practising your piece last night. Where did you leave it?'

'On the shelf. It's not there now.'

'What shelf are you talking about?' Penny apologised to the waiting mother. 'You couldn't possibly keep an eye on Lucetta for a moment?'

'I'll do it,' Elizabeth volunteered. 'Sorry,' she mumbled, and lowered her eyes to the floor, realising she was in disgrace.

Moments later she burst into laughter as Lucetta, anxious to re-establish her status as the centre of attention, jumped off her stool, landed in a puddle of water, and skidded across the kitchen floor, coming to land at the foot of a cupboard from where she proceeded to yap very loudly.

'If you can't find your recorder, you'll have to go to school without it, Elizabeth.' Penny said firmly. 'I haven't time to look for it.'

'The teacher will be ever so cross.' Elizabeth's blue eyes were now wide with anxiety.

'Then next time you'll take more care, won't you?' Penny replied in her no-nonsense voice.

Elizabeth swung her school bag over her shoulder. 'Here it is,' she said as she delved into its depths. 'It shifted to the bottom.'

'Thank goodness.' The waiting mother had been running out of patience. 'I'm late as it is.'

Barely pausing to blow her mother a kiss, Elizabeth ran out into the garden to join her classmates in the waiting vehicle parked in the lane.

'Come on, Lucetta.' Penny began to head for the day room. 'No, I am not carrying you.' After a few moments she was relieved to hear the patter of paws on the flagstones behind her. Lucetta had given in with dignity, and for that Penny was prepared to be forgiving. It wasn't her fault Lydia spoiled the dog, and she didn't want to do Lucetta an injustice by blaming her for all the little accidents that happened around her.

Her two part-time assistants were already busy shampooing the early arrivals. 'Hello, your ladyship.' Katy sketched a curtsey at Lucetta, then swept her up to give her a kiss, tickling the tender spot at the back of her neck. Lucetta arched her little body in delight and wriggled happily in Katy's arms.

'Lydia says we're to call her Miss Vale if we ring her at the studio today,' Penny informed the girls.

'I can think of a better name to call her. Sorry.' Katy grinned. 'Come on, Lucetta, let's get you lathered up.'

Leaving the girls to their duties, Elizabeth checked the schedule for the day. She was pleased to see no one had cancelled. With rumours running rife, she had expected one or two of her regulars to take their business elsewhere, but so far everyone had remained loyal. Penny's flexible approach was her unique selling point. She never made a fuss if clients were held up at work and late collecting their charges, and unlike her competitors, she didn't charge a cancellation fee if plans were changed at short notice.

The telephone rang on the desk. 'Penny's Parlour,' she answered the call. 'Penny speaking. How may I help you?'

'Are you free for lunch?' Roger asked.

'I am if you fancy stroking a dog for half an hour.'

'I beg your pardon?'

'It's very therapeutic.'

'I can't say it's anything I've ever done in my lunch hour before.'

'Then you haven't lived. You may be used to business lunches in your line of work, but I can't spare the time. What do you do, by the way?' Penny asked.

'I write motoring articles and reviews for the colour supplements.'

'If there's a snazzy sports number going spare, I'm up for it,' Katy said across the room, eavesdropping on the conversation.

Penny silenced her with a frown. 'Sorry,' she mouthed, not looking in the least repentant.

'Right, well, if you're on for a sandwich, ask Len to make me up a brownbread cheese and tomato with a side salad, no mayo, and bring along a couple of his freshly squeezed orange juices while you're at it. I'll see you at one.'

The two girls giggled as Penny hung up before Roger could object. 'So that's the celebrated Roger Oakes?' Nicole was agog with curiosity.

'He wants to do lunch,' Penny said.

'So we gathered.' Katy waved her dryer in the air and adjusted the settings. 'I wonder why he wants to see you.'

'Have you heard about Marika Wilczeski?' Penny asked. Both girls looked suitably intrigued. 'Roger Oakes is making plans for her to move into the farmhouse.'

'Does Lydia know?' Katy asked. 'Sorry. Is Miss Vale aware of this development?'

'Not unless Roger's told her.'

'Life is certainly getting exciting round here. There you are, Sophie. Fancy some cuddle time?' Nicole stroked her spaniel behind its left ear, something that always sent the dog into a paroxysm of delight. She whined in anticipation of further treats to come.

'Can I leave you two to run things?' Penny picked up her business file. 'I have to go to the bank, and then we need more supplies. I could be an hour or two.'

'Wondered why you were wearing your best skirt and smart blouse.' Nicole looked her up and down. 'You look the business. Good luck.'

Penny put her hand to her neck and

touched Steve's silver pendant. She didn't want to alarm the girls, but they must have suspected that even before this latest upset she had been struggling to cover costs. The business was thriving, but Penny always went the further mile, and that attention to detail was reflected in her lean profit margins. Things couldn't go on as they were.

'If you're not back by one, we'll eat your cheese and tomato,' Katy called after her.

'Then we'll set about Roger Oakes,' Nicole added.

With the strains of the gentle music of the relaxation tape following her outside, Penny clambered into her battered delivery van, which no matter how many air fresheners she purchased always managed to smell of damp dog.

The queue at the temporary traffic lights outside the new housing estate caused a long tailback, making Penny feel even more guilty for delaying the morning school run. Elizabeth wasn't a difficult child, but lately Penny sensed she was seeking attention. She was always a responsible child who responded well to being allocated small chores. Now, apart from her little patch of garden and collecting the hens' eggs, Elizabeth made a face whenever Penny suggested she prepare some vegetables or asked her to grate the cheese for the lasagne. Today's incident with her recorder was typical of her new behaviour pattern.

Penny was reluctant to have words with her, however. She didn't want a return to the traumatic days after Steve's accident, when Elizabeth began to sleepwalk and Penny was adjusting to her new life as a single parent, but something would have to be done if the situation continued.

Her parents would volunteer to help in a flash, but that would mean flying back from Spain to assist. They ran a bed and breakfast establishment for ex-pats on the Costa del Sol and could only conveniently get cover for a week or two. Penny knew they were always there for her, but they had their own lives to lead, and it wouldn't be fair to expect them to drop everything to come to her aid in what might prove to be a temporary crisis.

All the same, Penny was concerned. Elizabeth had settled in well at St Mary's. She had made new friends, and enjoyed her music practice and many after-school activities. Were her behavioural issues the start of another phase? As the queue of cars moved forward, Penny tried to convince herself it was nothing more than a blip, a situation that wasn't helped by the disruption of looking for new premises. She hoped her small-businesses manager would understand her problem, but she wasn't confident.

Road works and a bus breakdown further delayed Penny's journey, causing her to miss her allotted slot at the bank, entailing another half-hour's wait before she could be seen. As the rescheduled meeting progressed, she began to wish she hadn't bothered to wait for her appointment. Sean Turner painted a pessimistic picture regarding her loan if repayments should be withheld for longer than three months.

'But my business is thriving,' Penny said.

'I do understand, Mrs Graham, but when we agreed the terms of the loan you went to the limit of your credit. It would be difficult to extend it without incurring further penalty clauses, and frankly that is something I am reluctant to do bearing in mind your circumstances.'

'Circumstances?' Penny echoed. Her head was beginning to ache. Figure work was not one of her strengths, and she sensed she was fighting a losing battle.

'The arrangement you had with Ms Hyde was a very generous one. I understand she didn't charge you for the use of her premises.'

Penny shook her head. She could see what was coming.

'You don't need me to tell you that I don't think you'd be able to broker another such beneficial agreement.'

'Is that bank-speak for no loan extension?' Penny asked with a sinking heart.

'We do our best to encourage small businesses such as yours, but it would be irresponsible of us to set unrealistic targets.' Sean nudged his glasses further up the bridge of his nose. 'It's an unfortunate fact of life, but one should always make allowances for the unexpected.'

'Thank you for your help.' Penny gathered up her papers. There was no sense in prolonging the discussion.

'On a personal note . . . ' Sean looked more sympathetic now the business side of the meeting was over. He closed his file.

'Yes?' Penny queried.

'My aunt uses your facilities. Flora Clark?'

'The lady with the golden Labrador pup?'

'Dixie, that's right.'

'I'm not about to close up if she's

worried, Mr Turner,' Penny hastened to assure him.

'Please,' he insisted, 'no need to be so formal now our meeting's over. It's Sean.'

'Very well, Sean.' Penny wished he would be this nice when they were discussing business.

'Anyway,' Sean said when he'd finished beaming at Penny, 'my aunt has zillions of local contacts, and she's promised to put the word out among her friends and ladies' groups to see if anyone can provide suitable premises at a friendly rate. You never know, something may come up. Don't lose heart.'

'Thank you.' Penny smiled. 'I appreciate that.'

'My aunt would never forgive me if I didn't do my best to help. Please keep in touch.' They shook hands.

Outside on the pavement, the spring sunshine was doing its best to brighten up the day. Brave daffodils swayed on the village green, and purple primulas added a splash of colour to the newly dug bedding.

Penny began to walk along the pavement, but shoppers and the occasional client expressing concern over the situation at Cherry Tree Farmhouse impeded her progress. Flora Clark had indeed been busy spreading the word, and everyone had a take on Penny's situation and wanted to let her know their views. When Penny finally reached her grooming supplies retailer, she saw to her dismay a printed notice on the shop window informing customers that the premises were closed for the week due to staff holidays.

Fuming, she made her way back to the car and out towards alternative premises at the industrial unit. Yet again, the traffic lights held her up, and when she finally drew up outside the Cherry Tree Farmhouse the church clock was striking a quarter past one. A gleaming red Italian sports car was parked in the area Minnie had allocated for Penny's customers.

'Sorry,' Penny apologised to Katy and Nicole as she staggered into the day room, laden down with her purchases. She produced two bars of organic dark chocolate and handed them over.

'What's this, a bribe?' Katy asked.

'And what about our diets?'

Both girls immediately began to unwrap their treats.

'Anything to report?' Penny asked.

'Only that your visitor is on the patio,' Nicole informed her, adding, 'Have you seen his car?'

While they were talking, Penny did her best to repair the damage to her hair before she took on her next challenge of the day.

'How did it go with the bank?' Katy took another bite out of her chocolate bar.

'Much as I expected,' Penny replied. She had too much respect for the girls' integrity to mislead them in any way. 'Until things are sorted out, it's going to be a struggle.'

'We suspected as much,' Katy said through a mouthful of chocolate. 'Perhaps you ought to rethink your costs.'

'I hate to ask . . . ' Penny hesitated.

'But can we stay on?' Nicole threw her wrapper into the waste paper bin.

'For an hour?' Penny pleaded. 'Until Alice gets here.'

'What do you think?' Nicole looked at Katy.

'Only if weekly injections of organic chocolate are part of our new negotiated pay deal,' the other girl replied.

'Thanks, guys. You are stars.'

'Can we have that in writing?' Katy asked. 'Coming, my lovely,' she cooed to the rescue greyhound who had awoken from her sleep and was nervously blinking at her.

'Hurry up.' Nicole nudged Penny out of the door. 'Your cheese and tomato sandwich awaits.'

# 6

Roger got to his feet as Penny made yet another breathless late arrival. 'Got held up. Traffic lights,' she explained. 'Glad you didn't wait.' She eyed the sandwich wrapper, the half-eaten slice of cake, and the open carton of Len's orange juice on the wrought-iron table in front of Roger. 'And if you're going to make any remarks about how I should have made allowances for unforeseen circumstances, I've already had that lecture from the bank. And extra time wouldn't have done any good today because new traffic lights are popping up all over the place, so I never know how long it's going to take me to drive into town.'

Penny plonked down in the seat opposite Roger, then, barely pausing for breath, asked, 'Is that your red car outside parked in my customer-allotted parking space?' She undid the wrapping on her sandwich and took a healthy bite.

'My turn, is it?' Roger asked, taking advantage of the fact that Penny was temporarily unable to speak.

She put a hand over her mouth and tried to nod an apology for her outburst. When would she learn? Think first, speak second.

'If you want me to I will immediately move my car,' Roger offered, 'and I'm sorry if I've caused you any inconvenience.'

Penny shook her head. It wasn't her busy time, and it wasn't Roger's fault she'd had a bad morning. None of which she could say until she swallowed her mouthful of sandwich.

'Right, well I was delayed by traffic lights too, and if you look more carefully at the table you'll see I hadn't actually started my lunch. My sandwich is here, unwrapped but not eaten. I halved the cake; that's your slice over there. And I had only just undone my orange juice when you flew round the corner, so in the sandwich-eating stakes you are leading by a short length.'

'Sorry.' Penny managed to cough and clear her throat. 'It's been a busy morning. I had a frustrating interview at the bank, but I accept that's no excuse for speaking to you like that.'

'Apology accepted. How about we take a refreshment break before we get down to business?' Roger suggested with the semblance of a sympathetic smile.

'Good idea.' Penny eyed up Len's walnut and coffee gateau.

'That cake looks as though it'll do the job nicely,' Roger agreed. 'Len said I was to give you the biggest piece, so I've followed his instructions. And if you care to count the number of walnuts in your slice, you won't be disappointed.'

They ate in companionable silence. In the distance Penny could hear the trickling stream in the next field. The occasional passing of a car in the lane and the clip-clop of hooves towards the riding school at the top of the hill were the only other sounds to disturb their tranquillity. Penny eased her chair back into the sunlight as the early-afternoon shadows began to lengthen.

'Finished?' Roger asked.

Penny screwed her paper napkin into a ball and gave a satisfied sigh. 'Thank you,' she said, not sure what she was grateful for. 'I rushed out this morning without any breakfast. I can only put my bad manners down to lack of food.'

'Now we've put that problem out of the way — Marika.'

Penny's response was a guarded, 'Yes?' She began to suspect it might not have been such a good idea to eat so much walnut gateau. It churned in her stomach.

'She tells me she's reluctant to move into the cottage because you're making her feel unwelcome.' Roger held up a hand to stem Penny's interruption. 'A ghostly cavalier with an eye for the ladies?'

Penny could feel an ashamed flush staining her neck as the sun streamed down on her. 'I did intend to apologise, but after I'd collected Elizabeth and come back downstairs, you and Marika had gone out. Sorry.'

'It's not me you should be apologising to.' Roger waited patiently for Penny to go on.

'It's a story Minnie told me many times,' she said.

'Minnie was making it up.'

'How do you know?' Penny asked.

'My grandmother had a vivid imagination. She used to tell my mother fairies lived at the bottom of the garden, and when my mother expressed some scepticism, Minnie got the gardener to build a tiny hut and fashion wands out of twigs and stick stars on the ends of them.'

'How charming.' Penny broke into a smile. 'Isn't that just like Minnie?'

'Charming is not the reaction I was looking for,' Roger replied with a show of impatience.

'Are you sure you're Minnie's grandson?' Penny asked. 'You're not at all like her.'

'I don't think we need go down that route again. What I need to have is your assurance that you won't feed Marika any more silly stories about things that go bump in the night.'

'I never imagined Marika would be scared of a ghost.'

'Whereas you aren't?' Roger queried.

'If I did happen to come across an apparition with a feather in its hat, I'd give it what for.'

'That I don't doubt. But I'd rather Marika didn't tackle intruders of any nature.'

'Are the two of you an item?' Penny asked.

'Whatever gave you that idea?'

'She called you 'darling' and kissed you on the cheek.'

'She was being friendly, that's all.'

'I hope you don't expect me to follow her example.'

'We seem to be straying off the

point.' Roger looked rather red-faced.

Penny smiled. She quite enjoyed her exchanges with him; he was so easy to wind up. And from the alarmed look that had crossed his face when she had suggesting kissing him, she knew her words had hit their target. 'What I don't understand,' she said, 'is why you're trying to evict me from the theatre, but at the same time you invite someone you don't know to stay in the cottage.'

'I've said you can stay on for the time being, and I agree with John Warren that it's not a good idea for the house to stand empty. Marika comes with good references, so do you promise not to scare her with any more ghost stories?'

Penny nodded. 'It wasn't my intention to scare her, and I honestly didn't think she would take my words to heart.'

'She has a troubled family history. When she moved to this country, she hoped she would be able to settle, but things aren't working out as she hoped. Officialdom scares her, and when she got the letter from her landlord saying she would have to move out, she was really worried.'

Penny wriggled uncomfortably in her seat. By comparison, her troubles were minor. 'How did Marika find out about the cottage?' she asked.

'It was John Warren's idea.'

'John's a good friend,' Penny replied, remembering the times he had helped her when she and Elizabeth had first moved to St Mary's.

'Are you more than good friends?' Roger asked.

'John doesn't kiss me or call me 'darling', if that's what you mean.' Penny tossed back her hair, wishing it were long and sleek like Marika's and not curly blonde corkscrews. 'I could get Elizabeth to play her recorder for Marika one evening,' she offered by way of an olive branch, and in an attempt to change the subject.

'As long as Elizabeth doesn't mind.'

'She needs to practise, and I don't always have the time to listen. Marika would actually be doing me a favour.'

'Good, that's settled then.' Roger finished his orange juice. 'Now I'm sorry I can't stay on for dog-stroking duties, but I'm road-testing the car parked outside, and I'm on a deadline so I have to go. Was there anything else?'

Penny was sorely tempted to ask him to take her for a spin. She needed something to blow away the cobwebs fuddling her brain, but somehow she didn't think the car outside would do the trick. What she needed was physical exercise in the country. 'I suppose you wouldn't fancy a bike ride sometime?' she asked him.

Roger looked up from retrieving his keys from the pocket of his jacket.

'It's a healthy form of exercise. Much better than driving around in high-performance cars.'

'I haven't ridden a bicycle for years,' he admitted.

'Minnie stored her old one in the shed. It needs an overhaul, but I'm sure it's still up to the job. Elizabeth and I often ride out of a weekend if the weather's fine. I could show you the local countryside.'

'Perhaps I will join you.' A slow smile crossed Roger's face. 'Thank you.' If he tried, Penny thought, he could be quite attractive. Perhaps it was years of working to deadlines and writing reviews that had robbed him of a sense of fun.

Penny stayed where she was until the throb of Roger's twin exhausts had died away. Teasing Marika weighed heavily on her mind, and she would be glad to have the chance to make things up with her. She had no excuse for behaving so irresponsibly. If Marika thought playing up to Roger would get her a roof over her head, Penny had no right to judge her.

'Alice is here,' Nicole bellowed out of the day-room window. 'And if you're going to make us stay on any longer, we're putting in for more chocolate.'

Picking up the remains of their

lunch, Penny headed back to the office.

* ★ ★

An owl hooted from the copse at the back of the theatre. Penny pushed back the bed sheets. Sleep would not come. She got to her feet and, shrugging on her dressing gown, decided a cup of tea might ease her troubled mind.

Ghostly moonlight cast shadows across the garden, silhouetting Minnie's famous sculptures, all characters from her plays and modelled by one of her artistic gentleman friends. They had been a feature of the theatre tours that Minnie used to arrange from time to time, and visitors were fascinated to hear her tales from the stage no doubt suitably embellished. Roger had been right on that one — Minnie had a vivid imagination, and she liked to give it full rein when she was entertaining her guests.

Penny moved closer to the window, then blinked. One of the statues appeared to be moving. But that was impossible; they were solid bronze and fixed to pedestals.

'Elizabeth!' Penny's breath caught in her chest. She ran onto the landing and wrenched open her daughter's bedroom door, fearing she had started to sleepwalk again. But Elizabeth was sleeping peacefully in her bed.

Penny sagged against the doorframe. Then, gathering her wits, she crept down the stairs and grabbed a sturdy torch, careful not to make more noise than was necessary. She shivered as her breath misted the cold night air.

It may have been her imagination, and moonlight could play strange tricks, but Penny was convinced the shadow on the lawn had belonged to a living creature.

It couldn't possibly be Marika. She wouldn't move in at midnight, so she wasn't the cause of the disturbance. Penny strained her ears, trying to discern the direction of the night noises. The trees swayed gently in the air, and something small was rustling through the undergrowth in the field over the back — all noises Penny was accustomed to hearing. All the same, she couldn't shake off the suspicion that something wasn't right.

Switching on her torch and covering its glare with her hand, she crept round the back of the theatre past the day room. A grey shadow flitting past the picture window was briefly caught in the beam of her torchlight. Quelling the urge to confront the prowler, she sped back to her flat. This was a matter for the owner of the property. She dialled Roger's mobile number, intending to leave a message on his voice mail.

'Hello?' a sleepy voice answered.

'Roger, it's Penny. I'm sorry, I didn't mean to wake you up.'

'It's one in the morning.'

'I only wanted to tell you there's something going on at the cottage.'

'What sort of something?'

'I think there's an intruder.'

'If this is another ghost story,' he

said, sounding tetchy, 'I don't think it's very funny.'

'It's not. I couldn't sleep and at first I thought it was Elizabeth.'

'In the garden?'

'She used to sleepwalk.' Penny rushed on, reluctant to go into details. 'But she's asleep in bed. I did look outside . . . ' She got no further.

'Stay where you are and lock your door,' Roger replied. 'I'm coming straight over.'

# 7

Penny tied her dressing-gown cord tightly around her waist. The thought of Roger seeing her in her nightclothes was unnerving, but she didn't want to risk changing in case he arrived sooner than she had anticipated. The journey from The King's Head wouldn't take long at this time of night, and as the traffic lights were deactivated after four o'clock in the afternoon, there shouldn't be many hold-ups.

After doing another quick check to make sure Elizabeth was still asleep, Penny crept into the kitchen, filled the jug kettle with water, and plugged it in. A glance at the wall clock informed her it was now a quarter to two. It had been over twenty minutes since she had telephoned Roger. Doing her best to ignore the voice inside her head suggesting that perhaps he had gone back to sleep, she searched around for the teabags in an effort to take her mind off her current predicament.

Being town-bred, Penny still had difficulty acclimatising to the quiet of the countryside after nightfall. She had gradually grown used to animal noises and rustles in the undergrowth, although the first time she heard a vixen cry out she had thought someone was screaming at the top of his or her voice. When she'd raced over to tell Minnie to call the police, Minnie had laughed and suggested they have a glass of wine to soothe away her fears. Now when the wind and rain caused the trees to tap the window with their branches and create eerie patterns on the walls, it no longer worried Penny. What did worry her at the moment was the thought of a prowler up to no good. She began to wish Marika had moved into the cottage and that she could call on her for help.

The mug Penny was holding shattered to the floor as a loud shriek rent the air. She could not wait any longer for Roger. Grabbing a broom, she rushed outside. A stooped figure was hunched over the hencoop; and the hens, disturbed from their sleep, were clucking and running around in agitated circles.

'Get out of there!' Penny called out at the top of her voice, and lashed out with the wooden broom handle. There was a cracking sound. The pole made contact with something solid and the intruder fell to his knees. She advanced towards the prostrate figure groaning on the ground.

'You've dislocated my shoulder blade,' a voice gasped.

'Roger?' Penny's legs threatened to collapse under her.

'Put that thing down.' Still groaning, he rolled over and rubbed his shoulder.

'Are you all right?'

'Of course I'm not all right,' he snapped.

'What are you doing creeping around in the dark?'

'A fox was attacking the hencoop. Didn't you see it?'

'So that's what the shrieking was all about,' Penny breathed out in relief.

'You don't take prisoners, do you?' Roger was breathing heavily.

'How was I to know it was you?'

'An intelligent guess?'

'Where's your car?' Penny asked.

'I borrowed Len's bicycle.'

'Why?'

'I had no choice. The car was collected after I'd tested it. I had trouble unlocking his shed, that's what took me so long. Then when I caught the fox in the act of descending on your hens, I just went for it.'

'Are the hens all right?'

'They'll settle. And I'm fine too, thanks for asking.'

Penny stared at him, uncertain what to say.

'Why weren't you out here giving your nocturnal visitors what for?' he said. 'Or was that just talk about you not being scared of anything?'

'I, um, I didn't want Elizabeth upset, and I couldn't leave her alone in case she woke up and found me gone. Does that make sense?'

'Sort of,' Roger admitted.

'I'm not making excuses.'

Roger's voice softened. 'No one said you were.'

'Would you like a cup of tea?' Penny asked.

'That sounds like a plan.'

'It's why I got up in the first place. I couldn't sleep.'

Roger cast a last swift look at the hencoop to check everything was in order. 'You lead, I'll follow.'

Under the harsh strip lighting of the kitchen, Penny stifled a cry of shock. Roger was mud-spattered, his raincoat was damp with grass stains, and his pyjama collar was sticking out from under a jumper that had seen better days. 'Have you looked in the mirror?' she asked.

'You don't look so good yourself,' he retaliated.

'I didn't expect . . . I mean, your pyjamas?' She pointed to the evidence tucked into stout Wellington boots.

'The tone of your telephone call led me to believe it was an emergency. But if you're uncomfortable with such intimacy, I'll forego the tea. It's getting late anyway.'

A childish giggle from the doorway startled them. 'You look ever so funny.' Elizabeth put a hand over her mouth, her face screwed up with laughter. 'Doesn't he, Mummy?'

Penny whirled round. 'What are you doing up?'

'You were making a lot of noise shouting in the garden. Then I heard Hetty squawking. She's my favourite hen,' she explained to Roger. 'I thought if the fox was prowling around, I'd wake Mummy, but she wasn't in her bedroom. Then I heard voices in the kitchen and I saw the light on.'

'See?' Roger smiled at Elizabeth, then turned to Penny. 'Your daughter knew it was a fox. Whatever made you think it was a ghost?'

'I never said it was.'

'Were you trying to convince me Charles the cavalier really does exist?'

'Of course not.'

'There *is* a ghost.' Elizabeth was busy delving into the biscuit tin.

'How do you know?' Penny asked.

'Minnie told me.'

'Your grandmother has a lot to answer for,' Penny murmured to Roger under her breath. 'Pass the biscuits to our guest, Elizabeth.'

Elizabeth handed Roger the tin. 'Don't take the last chocolate finger.'

'Elizabeth,' Penny reprimanded her, 'Mr Oakes is a guest, and neither of you should be eating biscuits this late at night.'

With a joint show of defiance, both Roger and Elizabeth took a biscuit out of the tin.

'Oh, very well,' Penny gave in. 'I can't fight both of you. Elizabeth, would you like some hot milk to help you get back to sleep?'

'I'd like Roger to help me mend my bicycle chain.'

'It's Mr Oakes,' Penny said to her daughter.

'Roger's fine with me,' he insisted. 'What's all this about a bicycle chain?'

'It came off yesterday when I was wheeling it round the yard. I tried to put it back on but it was all loose.'

'I can't do anything about it now, but your mother's invited me for a bike ride at the weekend. Would that be soon enough? I've actually been getting in some practice tonight.'

'Fantastic.' Elizabeth snatched another biscuit before Penny replaced the lid.

'Drink up your milk,' Penny said, 'then back to bed. You've got school in the morning.'

'Is Marika coming to stay?' the child asked.

'We hope so,' Roger replied. 'Would you like that?'

'She can tell me all about her homeland for my geography project. Night, Roger. See you at the weekend.' Elizabeth blew him a kiss, then trundled back up the stairs.

'I hope she doesn't oversleep.' Penny began washing up the mugs. 'We were late for the school run this morning. Two days in a row and we might be banned from the rota.'

Roger wiped biscuit crumbs off the kitchen table. 'Right, well, I'll be off. We've had enough disruption for one night.'

'I should have realised it was a fox.'

'No harm done. Best get going. I have to be in London tomorrow.'

'I would drive you back, only I can't leave Elizabeth.' Penny hesitated. 'You can borrow my van if you like. Len's bike should fit in the back.'

'Not necessary. The exercise will do me good, and as long as I don't come across Charles I should be home within the hour. Check the chicken wire is mended properly in the morning. If there's a fox on the prowl, the running repairs I made won't stop it.'

'I'll get John to see to it,' Penny promised.

'By the way, Len's cleaning lady is

going to give the cottage the once-over before Marika moves in.'

'Have you mentioned anything to Lydia?'

'Should I?' Roger looked up from fastening the belt of his raincoat.

'It might be as well.'

'I haven't really spoken to her much at all.'

'She likes to be kept informed,' Penny said.

'When I get back from London I'll have a word with her. Make sure you lock the doors securely after I've gone.'

★   ★   ★

It seemed only moments later that Elizabeth was shaking Penny awake. 'Come on, Mummy. Nicole's already here. She made me some breakfast, and she says if you're not up in five minutes she's giving your toast to Dixie the Labrador.'

'I hear you had quite a party last night,' Katy said as Penny rushed into the day room.

'According to Elizabeth, you entertained Roger Oakes in his nightclothes.' Nicole raised her eyebrows. 'In the kitchen.'

'It wasn't like that.'

'You mean you weren't drinking tea and scoffing all the chocolate biscuits?' Katy looked disappointed.

'Well, yes we were,' Penny conceded. 'But Roger was wearing a raincoat over his pyjamas.'

'That's all right, then.' Nicole laughed.

'I beg your pardon?' a theatrical voice interrupted the exchange.

'Lydia,' Penny greeted her neighbour, wishing she hadn't chosen that moment to walk in on them. Lydia wasn't the most discreet of individuals. Rumours would be flying round St Mary's in no time at all.

'Did I hear you correctly? Roger Oakes was here after midnight in his pyjamas?'

'It isn't what you think,' Penny said.

'It never is.' Lydia looked ready to

believe the worst.

'Is there anything I can do for you?' Penny asked, doing best to divert the conversation to more innocent topics.

'I have a complaint.' Lydia made a sweeping gesture with her arms.

Penny's heart sank. When the mood was on her, Lydia could turn the slightest drama into a three-act play.

'I have had to take Lucetta to the vet.'

'Why?'

'Her infection has turned septic. The vet says if I'd left things any longer he might have had to operate.' Lydia shuddered.

'Are you saying one of us is responsible?' Katy asked.

'I'm not saying anything,' Lydia knew how to use her grey eyes and voice to full effect. The room fell silent.

'Then why are you telling us?' Penny asked.

'Because my pet insurance company has advised I put the matter in the hands of my solicitors if I wish to make a claim against my policy.'

'You're not serious.' It was Nicole's turn to protest.

'I would not joke about such matters.'

'Lucetta probably trod on a thorn,' Nicole insisted. 'She's very inquisitive.'

'You certainly know how to kick someone when they're down.' Katy's voice was full of disgust.

'I don't know what you mean,' Lydia blustered.

'Then let me make it clear to you.'

Penny knew she should stop Katy, but another disturbance in the doorway caught her attention.

'Penny's going to have to move out of the theatre because the cottage is up for sale,' Katy continued. 'She's been forced to take this action because you're interested in selling the land for development. Nicole and I will probably lose our jobs. Alice was getting over her agoraphobia nicely. Any relapses she may have will be your fault.'

'That's not how it is at all,' Lydia said.

'G'day. I hope I'm not interrupting things.' The new arrival was wearing black leggings and a white T-shirt, and had the skin texture of someone who spent long hours in the sunshine. All eyes swung in her direction. 'Sarah Deeds.' She smiled round the room. 'This is Cherry Tree Farmhouse?'

Penny found her voice. 'You're actually in the old theatre.'

'Then I'm in the right place, thank goodness. Had quite a trek finding it. I'd love a cup of tea.'

'Are you in need of pet-grooming services?' Penny asked.

Sarah burst into laughter. 'Look that bad, do I?' She ran a hand through her hair. 'I know I'm wrecked, but it's a long flight from Sydney.'

'You're Australian?' Nicole asked.

'Too right.'

'What are you doing here? It's miles from Sydney.'

Sarah broke into laughter. 'What a homecoming this is turning out to be. I'm Minnie Hyde's granddaughter.'

# 8

'I got delayed — a charity yogathon on Bondi Beach.' Sarah looked round for confirmation and support. 'Otherwise I would have been here sooner.' Her beaming smile encapsulated the whole room. Everyone was staring at her with open mouths. Not in the least daunted by her reception, she carried on. 'Do you know what Bondi means in Abo?' she asked, the cheerful expression on her face not faltering.

Nicole was the first to recover some semblance of her usual her voice. 'I can't say I do.'

'It's water over rocks. So hey, you've learned something new today.' She stifled a yawn. 'Sorry, jet-lagged. Anybody here related to Minnie?'

'No, we're not,' Katy replied.

'That's a pity.'

'But we all knew her.' Nicole nodded

with enthusiasm.

'That's great. The solicitor guy told me I had a cousin, name of Roger Oakes? Guess none of you ladies fit that description.'

'You can't be Minnie's granddaughter,' Lydia croaked, sounding outraged at the very idea.

Sarah's deep-set blue eyes widened as she took in the pearls and the sequinned top. 'You look kind of a grand lady. Should I curtsey?'

Nicole did her best to disguise an unladylike snigger.

'I believe in looking my best.' Lydia tilted her chin at the newcomer.

'Too right,' Sarah agreed. 'Great to meet you, and I assure you I *am* Minnie's granddaughter. What's more, I can prove it.'

'You can?' Lydia blinked in confusion.

'Even if the call hadn't gone out for rellies, I was going to come over to the old country to pay my respects to the family.' For the first time Sarah's smile slipped. 'But it looks like I'm too late.'

'How old are you?' Lydia asked, displaying an unusual lack of tact.

'Fifty-five,' Sarah replied. 'And since we're on the subject, how old are you?'

Penny turned her laugh into a hasty cough. Lydia's age was a closely guarded secret, but Minnie happened to let slip one day that she was only two years older than 'that nosey parker next door'. It hadn't taken a degree in rocket science to work out that Lydia's publicity handout was not entirely accurate when it came to the year of her birth. But in deference to Lydia's dignity, Penny had always maintained a discreet silence on the matter.

'Minnie had a daughter, Freya, by her second husband, and Roger Oakes is Freya's son,' Lydia said, swiftly deflecting the conversation away from the delicate subject of her age.

'My father was Henry Deeds,' Sarah said.

'Minnie had a child by Geoffrey Deeds?' Lydia repeated in amazement.

'He was her first husband, right?' Sarah asked.

'It can't be true.' Lydia was still in denial.

'Why not?' Sarah looked interested.

'The age gap, it's all wrong. I mean, Roger's years younger than you.'

'And Henry was years older than Freya, but hey, who's counting?' Sarah shrugged. 'Let's get down to business. You all know who I am. How about an introduction?'

'My name is Lydia Gerard. Desmonde Vale was my professional name.' Lydia paused as if waiting for recognition from Sarah. When there was no response, she continued, 'Minnie and I were contemporaries.'

'You act too?'

'I was classically trained.'

'Then you will have known Geoffrey, my grandfather, professionally?'

Lydia was still looking numbed with shock. 'I really can't remember.'

'Well, there you have it. Dad left for Australia as a young man. He married my mother after he arrived in Sydney, but he couldn't settle. He went to live in the outback. We didn't hear much from him after that. From what you tell me, he wasn't hot at keeping in touch with any of the family.'

'How sad,' Penny said. She couldn't imagine losing touch with Elizabeth, no matter what the circumstances.

'Did Minnie have any other children?' Nicole looked intrigued.

'I truly have no idea,' Sarah replied. 'I discovered some old paperwork amongst my mother's effects. There was a photo of a baby and the name on the back said Freya. I guess that must have been Roger's mother?'

Penny nodded.

'Then I saw the internet search for Minnie's descendants. Her bio said she'd been married to Geoffrey Deeds, and I knew he was my grandfather, so I worked out that this Freya had to be related to Dad, and it turns out she was his sister. How about that?'

'It's like something out of a film,' Katy said. 'A long-lost granddaughter.'

'This is great,' Sarah enthused. 'I've never married and I'm an only child. When I lost my mother, I thought I had no one left in the world. But it turns out I've got a cousin I knew nothing about, and all you lovely ladies.'

'We're not related to Minnie,' Penny reminded her.

'But you're a bond with Minnie. Sorry, sweetie, I don't know your name.'

'Penny Graham. I rented the theatre from Minnie. My daughter Elizabeth and I live in the accommodation above the theatre. I run a pet-grooming parlour.'

'Not for much longer,' Nicole reminded her.

'Why's that?' Sarah asked.

'We're being evicted,' Katy said.

'Say, not because of me?' Sarah looked distressed.

'Your cousin Roger is hoping to sell up,' Katy told her. 'Lydia owns half the land and she has plans to develop the site.'

Lydia flushed. 'I'm sure Ms Deeds doesn't want to be bothered with all that now,' she said in a rush.

'I'm sure I do,' Sarah insisted with a smile.

'The solicitors will have all the details,' Lydia replied. 'Why don't you have another word with them?'

'It looks like my arrival has put the cat among the pigeons.'

'And some,' Nicole agreed.

A silence fell on the gathered group as they took stock of the situation.

'Were you looking for Roger?' Penny finally asked.

'The solicitor thought he might be here,' Sarah replied.

'He's gone to London.'

'No worries. I'm rooming at The King's Head.'

'So is Roger.'

'Then I'll bump into him before long I suppose.'

'How long are you planning on

staying?' Lydia asked.

'I've an open return ticket, so I don't have any definite plans right now.'

'There's something else you ought to know,' Penny volunteered.

'What's that?' Sarah asked.

'Roger's made temporary arrangements for a friend to live in the cottage.'

Lydia swung round to confront Penny. 'No one told me anything about this.'

'If you're asking for my permission, I don't mind,' Sarah put in.

'Penny doesn't have any say in the matter,' Lydia snapped. 'She doesn't own the farmhouse.'

'Neither do you,' Nicole pointed out.

Fed up with being ignored, Lucetta gave a short sharp bark.

'Say, is that a Shih Tzu?' Sarah leaned forward and tickled Lucetta's neck. The dog gave another friendly yelp. 'My you are a beautiful baby.'

Lydia's expression softened. 'Lucetta has a pedigree.'

'She's also carrying a few extra

pounds,' Sarah said. 'How about we go for a walk, Lucy? Get out of everybody's hair?'

'Lucetta,' Lydia corrected her.

Lucetta wagged her tail and gazed adoringly at Sarah.

'OK, Lucetta. Are you on for some exercise?'

'Lucetta isn't booked in for the day.' Lydia scooped her up.

'Did you cut your paw?' Sarah touched the bandage. Lucetta licked her hand and whined.

'Lydia says it's our fault,' Katy put in.

'You don't say.' The sunny expression on Sarah's face slipped. 'Have you been telling tales?' She tickled Lucetta under the chin.

'Come along, Lucetta. Time for your elevenses.' Lydia swept out of the day room, carrying a wriggling Lucetta in her arms.

Sarah watched them leave. 'She and Minnie really were neighbours? I guess they had quite a few battles.'

'Minnie gave as good as she got,' Penny assured the Australian woman. 'Although she never would have admitted it in a million years, I think it energised her.'

'Minnie sounds my sort of girl.' Sarah's sunny smile was back in place. 'Say, is there anything I can do to make myself useful? I hate sitting around doing nothing. How about exercising the clients?'

'Alice is due in later.'

'She's Len's daughter, right? She was telling me about her agoraphobia. Poor kid. I'd like to help.'

'She started dog-walking as therapy, and she's almost cured,' Penny explained.

'That's another reason we don't want to leave,' Katy said.

'I'm on side with that one,' Sarah said. 'Fresh air and exercise is the best thing for Alice. We can't let Roger and Lydia ruin her life.'

'Hold on,' Penny cautioned. 'We're not there yet.'

'You're right,' Sarah agreed. 'I spoke

without thinking. Blame it on the family genes.'

'Come on, Katy,' Nicole urged. 'We'd best get on.'

'I'm very good at cleaning,' Sarah volunteered. 'Do you have a spare pair of rubber gloves?'

'You don't have to,' Penny insisted.

'Yes she does,' Nicole butted in. 'I want to hear all about koalas and kangaroos and crocodiles.'

'And Sydney Harbour Bridge.' Katy looked expectantly at Sarah. 'Is it true you have spiders that spit?' she asked.

'You don't get too much of that where I come from. Although a bite from the Sydney funnel web can be nasty if not treated in time.'

'Have you been to the Great Barrier Reef?' Nicole asked.

'I've been snorkelling off Northern Queensland. It's beautiful up there. The fish are breathtaking and some even swim alongside you. The coral is dazzling, like the Crown Jewels, but you have to go and see for yourself.' Sarah began tying an apron around her waist. 'OK, guys. Put me to work. I'll tell you all about the coral reef another time. How about we arrange a hen night? Get some of the gang together? We could all chillax and get to know each other better.'

Katy and Nicole immediately fell in with Sarah's suggestion and began making plans.

'Well if you don't mind helping out,' Penny gave in, 'I'll leave Katy and Nicole to show you the ropes. I'll be in the office if you need me, girls.'

For the rest of the day a constant stream of visitors dropped by to inspect the new arrival. Sarah's outrageous stories had everyone doubled up, and the day room rang with laughter. She proved a natural with another group of senior citizens who arrived after their lunch at The King's Head, and by the end of the afternoon, Penny, who had joined them, was exhausted from serving up vast quantities of tea and cakes.

'So, put your feet up,' Sarah insisted after everyone had gone and she and Penny had the parlour to themselves. 'When do I get to meet your daughter? Elizabeth, wasn't it?'

'It's recorder practice today,' Penny explained. 'Elizabeth is due to play in the school concert so she won't be home until later. Her teacher usually drops her off.'

'Tell me if I'm speaking out of turn.' Sarah poured out two mugs of tea. 'But are you a single parent? I won't take offence if you don't want to answer that question. Us nosey Aussies have skins as tough as a crocodile's.'

'Yes, I am a single parent,' Penny admitted. 'Steve, my husband, worked in the oil industry.' Her voice gave out. 'Sorry, I'm not used to talking about him.'

'Then you don't have to,' Sarah insisted.

'I'd like to,' Penny said, warming to the Australian girl.

'Great, well, fire away, I'm a good listener.'

'Steve had the chance to work abroad. Elizabeth was growing up and our flat was far too small for us as a family, so we agreed between us he would do an extra tour of duty to get a bonus. We planned to move out of the city into the country.'

'I get the picture.' Sarah squeezed Penny's hand.

'Steve loved water sports. He was always very careful, but one day he lost his balance and hit his head.'

'And to think I went on about snorkelling on the Great Barrier Reef. How thoughtless was that? Sweetie, I must apologise.'

'You weren't to know. Anyway, after that I couldn't stay in London, but I didn't know what to do. Then I saw Minnie's advert for a companion. The set-up she proposed fitted in with my plans, and the next thing I knew we were in. We've been so happy here.'

'Tell me about Minnie.'

'Did you never have the desire to be an actress?' Penny asked.

Sarah raised her eyebrows. 'No way. I'm a fitness instructor. I love the open air. I couldn't work in a theatre to save my life. I'm a sunshine girl. I help out occasionally at my local sportswear store, and I have a friend who runs a knick-knack shop — you know, selling beads, aromatic candles, that type of thing. It's a great life.'

'Minnie liked the outdoor life too. She was always in the garden tending her roses, and would work outside no matter the weather or the time of day. She'd drive Lydia mad working by torchlight after it got dark. And she used to wear this funny hat thing with a light on it. The first time I saw her, it gave me quite a shock, I can tell you. Lydia often came storming over saying Minnie was keeping her awake, and they'd have a lovely argument, then the next thing I knew they were opening a bottle of wine and exchanging outrageous stories.'

'I liked Lydia. She has standards.'

Sarah laughed. 'Does she have any family?'

'Her late husband Liam was an artist. Minnie told me he wanted her to sit for him, and one day Lydia discovered the pair of them together in his studio. Liam was placing purple combs in Minnie's hair. I don't know the details, but Minnie said Lydia didn't speak to her for ages after that. Of course, I don't know if the story's true.'

'Sounds like Minnie knew how to spin a good tale.'

'I actually think she and Lydia kept each other going, and the reason Lydia's making a nuisance of herself now is because she's lonely.'

'I know how she feels.'

'You do?' Penny said, surprised.

'That's why I came over here. I knew I had family in this country. I wanted to trace my roots, find out who I am.'

'I wonder why Minnie didn't keep in touch with Henry.'

'We don't know that she didn't. But as I said, my father wasn't the best at letter-writing, and in those days that was about the only form of communication between here and Australia. I did find a brooch that I think might have belonged to Minnie, though. It wasn't the sort of thing my mother would have worn, but perhaps an actress would. It's back in my room. I'll show it to you sometime.'

Penny finished up the last of the cake that she and Sarah had managed to snaffle from the refreshment tray before their guests had departed.

Sarah stood up. 'That sounds like Alice and the dogs coming back, so I guess that's my signal to leave. Len's picking us up. Don't forget our date. Arrange something with the gals and we'll have a real good night out.'

Penny sat where she was for several minutes after Sarah and Alice had left, trying to get her head around all that had happened. Without his cousin's agreement, would Roger be allowed to sell out to Lydia? And what if there were more claimants? With Minnie, anything was possible.

Penny shook her head before crossing to the window. The sun was setting and the hens needed to be locked up. Elizabeth would never forgive her if anything happened to Hetty, and she would never forgive herself if the fox attacked the others.

# 9

Roger was dressed in jeans and a sweatshirt and holding up a carrier bag. 'Are we still on for it?' he asked.

Penny frowned, not sure what he was talking about.

'You promised me a bike ride, remember? I've brought a can of oil to squirt at rusty chain links and anything else that looks as though it needs reviving. If you show me where Minnie kept her boneshaker, I'll have a go at that too.'

The May sunshine poured through the open window of the living room. Roger looked at Penny's open laptop on the desk and the papers scattered over the carpet. 'You're not working at the weekend are you?' he said.

'No. Everyone's got the day off today.'

'Except you.'

'I'm still trying to make sense of my figures.'

'Then a bout of fresh air is what you need to clear your head. And we did have a date, didn't we?'

'I forgot. I'm sorry,' Penny admitted.

'I should have rung up to confirm, but I only got back late last night. So after breakfast I decided to come on over. Where's Elizabeth?'

'If she's not egg-collecting or playing with Hetty, she'll be in the rose garden.'

'No more visits from Mr Fox?'

Penny shifted uncomfortably in her seat. She still wasn't entirely sure Roger believed her garbled explanation about an intruder. 'I hope you scared him away.'

'How about a cup of coffee before we get going?' Roger suggested. 'I could make it if you like.'

'There's a tin of biscuits on the top shelf.'

'I suppose you put them there so I couldn't get my hands on the chocolate fingers?' Penny began to deny the accusation but Roger ignored her. 'I can be trusted not to pinch them all, you know.'

'I put them up there because they aren't safe from Bracken.'

'Is anything?'

'He's not keen on fruit and vegetables, but anything sweet and he's there like a shot.'

Roger reached up for the tin. 'Found them. Now what?'

'Mugs?'

'I understand you've met Sarah.' Roger's voice was muffled as he disappeared into the depths of the crockery cupboard.

'I have.' Penny unscrewed the jar of coffee.

'Sarah tells me she's met Lydia too.'

'I don't know if she was more annoyed to learn of Sarah's existence or the fact that Minnie never told her she had a son.' Penny flicked the switch on the kettle.

'It came as something of a shock to

me too.' Roger put the mugs down on the table.

'You didn't know about Henry?'

'I'd never heard of him, and I don't recall my mother mentioning a brother.'

'Do you think she's genuine?' Penny felt forced to ask.

'Sarah showed me her photograph of my mother. It certainly looks real. It's with the solicitors now. She's also got a brooch that she thinks might be a family heirloom. We'll have to wait and see how things pan out.' A rueful smile quivered at the corners of Roger's mouth. 'You must think we're a very odd family, no one knowing about anyone else.'

Penny shook her head, uncertain what to say.

'My mother died when I was twelve,' Roger said. 'And my father ... I suppose you could say he went into his shell. He hardly talked about her. Then we went abroad to live. It's not surprising we all lost touch.'

'I have a half-sister who's eleven

years older than me,' Penny said. 'We get on well when we meet up, but our lives have gone in different directions. She lectures on philosophy.'

'And you run a pets' parlour.'

'Exactly.' She poured hot water over the coffee granules.

Roger picked up his cup with an appreciative sniff. 'Len has many good qualities, but coffee-making is not one of them.'

'What will you do now?' Penny asked.

'I'll stay on for the time being, if that's all right with everyone.' Roger looked expectantly at Penny.

'It's hardly my place to say,' Penny replied, surprised to realise how glad she was that he wasn't leaving.

'It is your business in a way.'

'How come?'

'Sarah's not sure she wants to sell up, and I'd need her agreement to do anything if her claim is found to be genuine. The outcome could affect your position here.'

'Where is Sarah?'

'She and Alice have gone out for the day.'

'Len must be delighted,' Penny said with genuine pleasure. 'Alice hasn't had a panic attack since she started dog-walking. He used to beg Alice to go out for the day with him but she wouldn't.'

'I think that may be what's influenced Sarah against selling up. She feels any change might undo everyone's good work.'

'What about Marika?' Penny asked. 'I've heard nothing from her either.'

'She'll be over sometime this weekend. John has promised to drive her. I need to double-check a few things first — electricity and water, things like that — but it looks as though she's another one who can stay as long as she likes.'

'Have you spoken to Lydia?'

Roger grimaced. 'Not yet, but the solicitors have been in touch and they tell me she doesn't seem too fussed about the delay this will cause. She's probably thriving on all the gossip. Anyway,' Roger added, finishing his coffee, 'shall we check out the transport?'

'Get Elizabeth to show you the shed. I'll make up some sandwiches for the trip.'

'How far were you thinking of going?' Roger looked mildly concerned. 'It took me ages to cycle home the other night. I'm still saddle sore.'

'But you got the hang of it, didn't you?'

'Maybe, but I'm not up to Tour de France standard yet.'

'I thought perhaps we could go up to the tower.'

'That sounds as though it's on a hill.' Another anxious look crossed Roger's face.

'It is. The smugglers used it as a lookout post for revenue men and soldiers when they were owling.'

'When they were whatting?'

'Owling — the illegal trafficking of wool. Ask Elizabeth to tell you all about it. She did a project on local history. She and Minnie made up a story about smugglers and soldiers, and illustrated it with tufts of wool and scraps of silk. I steamed the label off a jar of hot chocolate for them. It was good stuff, very colourful. Minnie was thrilled to bits when she and Elizabeth were awarded a gold star. She said it meant more to her than all her acting accolades.'

Penny smiled at the memory of a blushing Minnie accepting her certificate at the local school. The children loved her, and afterwards she had kept them royally entertained with stories about her life on the stage.

'Right, well, I'd better attend to my duties.' Roger picked up his can of oil. 'I may be some time,' he added.

As Penny cut the sandwiches, Elizabeth's laughter floated up from the rose garden. She peered out of the window. Roger was doing his best to mend the chain on the old bicycle. His wispy hair was coated in oil, and from the grim expression on his oil-streaked face, Penny surmised that all was not going well.

A shadow fell across the lawn and a husky voice interrupted the scene. 'Darling, what do you do?'

'Who are you?' Elizabeth asked, her hands on her hips as she confronted the newcomer.

A tall figure bent down to speak to the child. 'Hello, darling. My name is Marika. I have come to move in to the cottage. See, here are all my things.'

John now appeared behind her, carrying a box and a bag. 'Hi there, Princess,' he said. 'Marika's going to be your new neighbour.'

'You're the lady who's going to hear me play my recorder, aren't you?' Elizabeth looked suitably awestruck.

Marika was wearing a deep maroon dress and matching felt hat. Her long, dark hair hung in ringlets down her back. 'I would be honoured to listen to you play.'

'Mummy says she's sorry she told

you ghost stories.' Elizabeth giggled. 'She got paid back because when the fox tried to attack the hens, she thought it really was a ghost, and she had to call for Roger to come and rescue her.'

Everyone broke into laughter. Penny flushed. 'Serves me right,' she muttered under her breath. 'Listeners never hear any good of themselves.'

She ducked down out of sight before anyone spotted her peering out of the window. She would be having words with her daughter about being rescued by Roger. It was a story that needed to be nipped in the bud. Being rescued by men was not her style. Wrapping up the sandwiches, Penny made her way downstairs.

To her surprise, Marika greeted her with a kiss on the cheek. 'There you are. Your daughter has been keeping us entertained with stories of things that go bump in the night. I hope you have not had any more visitations?'

'Hello everyone,' a voice rang out. Penny groaned and Roger ducked down behind Minnie's bike. Lydia was delicately picking her way across the lawn in heels that were most unsuitable for walking on damp grass. Lucetta sniffed Marika's stylish red leather boots. Penny was relieved to see the dog wasn't limping and that her wound was healing well.

'Hello, Mrs Gerald,' Marika replied, towering over their neighbour.

'It's Ms Gerald, actually. I kept my maiden name when I married dear Liam, but call me Lydia please,' she insisted.

'I hope then, Lydia, you have no objection to me moving in?'

'None at all,' Lydia answered smoothly. She inspected the gathered throng. 'Can I help in any way?'

'How good are you at mending bicycle chains?' Roger asked.

'Absolutely hopeless,' Lydia admitted.

'I suppose with those nails it's no good asking you to help me unload the van either,' John said.

Lydia cast him a disparaging look. 'You still haven't finished your work on my patio, young man.'

'All in good time,' he said. 'You're next on my list. Now I haven't got all day to stand around chatting.'

'I'll help you, darling.' Marika hastened after John.

'I like Marika,' Elizabeth announced. 'Shall I go and fetch my recorder now?'

'What about our bike ride?' Roger asked.

'You're very slow mending my chain,' Elizabeth complained, 'and you haven't got all the cobwebs off Minnie's bike.'

'How about lending a hand, Lydia?' Penny asked. 'I could let you have a bucket and a sponge.'

The grey eyes turned frosty. Penny suspected Lydia's impromptu visit was not going as planned. 'I was hoping to have a word with Sarah,' Lydia admitted.

'She is staying at the King's Head. Maybe you find her there,' Marika suggested as she deposited a box of her

142

belongings on the lawn, clearly unaware of the story of Lydia being banned from the premises after she had a monumental falling out with Len over the quality of his coffee and the standard of his cooking.

Lydia ignored Marika and addressed her remarks to Roger. 'Perhaps you could pass on a message? I've a meeting scheduled with a development representative and I wondered if Sarah would like to attend.'

It was as if a chill had descended on the garden. 'Then you're going ahead with your proposal?' Penny asked.

'I'm making preliminary enquiries,' Lydia admitted. She glanced at the cottage. 'You have to admit the building is in a sorry state, and frankly I don't think it's saleable in its current condition.' The 'For Sale' sign had been taken down by the estate agency at Roger's request and with the solicitors' agreement.

'Aren't you getting ahead of yourself, Lydia?' Roger asked.

'I don't think so.'

'We all know Sarah is reluctant to sell, and whatever action is taken has to be agreed by the two of us.'

'Maybe I can persuade her to change her mind,' Lydia said.

'Get out the way, Lucetta!' John shouted at Lydia's dog. 'You'll have me over. Can't you control your animal, Lydia?' He juggled with the box he was holding as he manoeuvred his way through the gate.

'Stop shouting at her, John. You know Lucetta doesn't like people raising their voices.'

'Look out!' John tried to stop a madly barking Lucetta rushing past him and out into the lane. There was a loud squeal of brakes.

'Lucetta!' Lydia raced across the lawn as fast as her heels would allow.

John grinned as the sound of a heated exchange with the male car driver floated over the hedge. Lucetta sauntered back through the gate, looking as though butter wouldn't melt in her mouth.

'Lucetta,' John said with a wink at the dog, 'I like your style.'

A red-faced Lydia emerged from behind the hedge and slammed the gate shut. Having lost out in her verbal battle with the van driver, she transferred her annoyance to Marika. 'Rules of the country — always close the gate.'

'I did not leave it open. And, second rule of the country,' Marika retaliated, 'always check it's properly shut.'

In her haste to close the gate, Lydia had not realised it was not latched onto its hinge. It creaked, then slowly swung open again. Lucetta began trotting towards the gap. 'No!' Lydia roared, and scooped her up.

John laughed as the dog poked her head over Lydia's shoulders. 'I'm really bonding with Lucetta today.'

Penny joined in with his laughter. 'Did you see her wink?'

'Mummy,' Elizabeth squealed, 'Lucetta's paw is much better. She ran across the lawn ever so fast.'

'And I think I've sorted Elizabeth's

chain.' Roger did a few experimental spins of the wheel. 'So if we're all set?'

'Where're you off to?' John enquired.

'The tower,' Elizabeth replied. 'Then we're going to eat our sandwiches and freewheel all the way down the hill. It's much easier coming down than going up.'

'Rather you than me.' John slapped Roger on the back. 'I bet Penny didn't tell you Minnie's bike is a death trap. The basket has a will of its own, and the pedals have this tendency to go in different directions.' He grinned. 'But don't let me put you off. You'll have a great time.'

'See you later, darlings.' Marika blew everyone a kiss. 'I have my first-aid badge if anyone gets into trouble.'

The trio wheeled their bikes across the lawn and down towards the gate, which Roger closed behind them with exaggerated care. Then he mounted Minnie's bike and began to wobble down the lane.

# 10

'Chill.' Alice sketched a smiley emoticon on one of Len's paper serviettes and pushed it towards Penny. 'There's no need to look so worried.'

'I can't help feeling twitchy,' Penny said to Alice, who was wearing one of her more colourful Goth outfits — a black and purple T-shirt, a leather skirt, and tights that looked as though they had been fashioned from spider webs.

'You don't get out enough, that's what's wrong with you.'

'I know. I promise to do better,' Penny replied. 'And hark who's talking,' she teased.

Alice flushed. 'I've been thinking of going back to college in the autumn,' she confided.

'That's brilliant.' Penny hugged her.

'Mind Dad's decorations,' Alice protested as the two of them came perilously close to knocking over a jug of water.

Penny sat down again, still smiling. 'You're sure Elizabeth is settled?' She sipped some of the water she had almost upset.

'She's playing a game on my console. She's had some of Dad's special fish fingers for tea, with red jelly and ice-cream for afters. She knows where we are, and the girls in the kitchen have promised to keep an eye on her during their break. She'll be spoilt rotten.'

'Then the only thing I have left to worry about is Lydia. I hope she won't make a scene.'

'Dad's lifted his ban, but she knows she's for the red card if there's any trouble.'

The rest of their party was sorting out bags and coats. Len had offered them the use of The King's Head's private lounge for their night out, and every facility to be at their disposal. Penny wasn't sure how Lydia had gate-crashed the party, but no one had dared object.

'She's certainly glammed up,' Alice said. 'The last time I saw that many sparkles, they were on a Christmas tree.'

Lydia beamed at the girls as everyone eventually settled down. Having manoeuvred herself a seat at the head of the table, she was now ready to control the proceedings. 'I hope no one minds,' she gushed, 'but I've ordered a bottle of fizzy wine to mark the occasion.'

'Good on you, Lids.' Sarah slapped her on the back. 'And as no one's driving, I suggest we make an evening of it and have a bottle of Australian white to follow.'

Sarah looked equally stunning in a leopard-skin print top, black leggings, and inches of native Australian bracelets on her wrists. They jangled against each other as she clapped her hands for quiet. 'Lids has something to say,' she announced.

Lydia raised her glass. 'I would like to propose a toast to absent friends.'

Penny was glad Lydia hadn't mentioned Minnie by name. There were ongoing issues still to be resolved regarding Cherry Tree Farmhouse, and whilst everything had gone quiet for the moment, she didn't want the slightest spark to set things off. When the mood was on them, Nicole and Katy didn't require much stimulation to stir things up.

'And please, no talk about Charles the ghostly Cavalier.' With a twinkle in her eye, Marika flashed Penny a telling look.

It was Penny's turn to blush as everyone laughed. 'You have my word.'

★ ★ ★

It had taken Marika the whole of the previous weekend to move in. 'I didn't realise she had quite so much stuff,' John complained as he made yet another trip in his van. 'Not sure Roger did either.'

'The boxes contain my early-autumn

collection,' Marika explained. 'I have to store them somewhere. There are too many people in the shop and things become misplaced. Then I panic.'

'Autumn? It's only May,' John protested.

Both Penny and Marika threw him a pitying glance. 'What?' he asked.

'Fashion always works ahead of season,' Penny explained.

'Well how was I to know?' John grumbled, lugging more packing cases into the cottage. 'Reckon you've got enough clothes for all four seasons in here.'

Marika sniffed. 'Can you smell damp?' she asked. 'I must have dry storage, otherwise the collection will be ruined.'

'Perhaps if we opened a window or two,' Penny suggested. 'Let some air through.'

Penny had helped Marika store her boxes in Minnie's cupboards, after which they'd enjoyed a pasta supper while Elizabeth played to them on her recorder. Companionable evenings in the cottage had been something Penny and Elizabeth had missed, and they all hoped that evening would be the first of many. Marika proved an entertaining companion, telling them about life on the catwalk and the antics of the fashion industry.

'You come from Crack Cow don't you?' Elizabeth asked as she put away her recorder.

'Cracow,' Marika corrected her gently. 'I have postcards and pictures somewhere.'

'I've decided Crack Cow is going to be my next project. Minnie helped me with the last one. We got a gold star.'

'I think it would be polite to first ask Marika nicely if you'd like some help with your project,' Penny said. 'She's very busy.'

'Not too busy to help, but only if you learn to pronounce Cracow properly, darling.'

'I will,' Elizabeth promised solemnly. 'I want to hear about Australian wildlife. You promised,' Nicole reminded Sarah as they nibbled on some savoury canapés that Lydia had produced from a cold bag.

'That's a tall order! I don't know where to start,' Sarah laughed. 'Has anyone here ever visited my part of the world?'

'I once did a tour down under with a travelling rep company,' Lydia announced. She closed her eyes. 'The heat was unbearable.' She put a hand to her forehead as if simulating a feeling of fatigue. Katy and Nicole looked ready to start laughing. 'We had to wear heavy costumes and the wigs gave everyone headaches. I remember on one particular occasion . . . ' she began.

Penny's attention wandered. When Lydia started on her stories, it was impossible to interrupt. She hoped the girls wouldn't fidget too much.

'Dad's done us proud, wouldn't you say?' Alice murmured in Penny's ear as their starter platters began arriving.

'Salmon mousse, then Mediterranean casserole to follow; and if anyone's got room, strawberry tarts to finish.'

'What does he put in the casserole?' Penny inhaled the fragrant steamy aroma rising from the serving dish on the sideboard.

'Anything he can find.' Alice grinned. 'But hey, enough of the domestic stuff. How was your bike ride with Roger?'

'That man is a fraud,' Penny said firmly.

'Keep your voice down,' Alice urged.

'Well he is,' Penny hissed.

'What'd he do?' Alice grinned. 'Swindle you out of the best saddle?'

'He knew all along how to ride a bike.'

'I know. He borrowed Dad's contraption the other night when you called him out.'

Did everyone know about that episode? Penny thought in frustration. 'He should have told me.'

'Told you what?' Alice looked confused.

'That he was good at it.'

'What's got into you?' Alice regarded Penny in surprise.

'He raced up to the tower, then laughed because Elizabeth and I were knackered.'

'I bet he ate all the sandwiches too. Men, you just can't trust 'em.'

Penny gave a shamefaced smile. 'We all made short work of them,' she admitted. 'It's hungry work, riding a bike.'

'Did you enjoy his company?'

'Roger's?'

'Who else did you think we were talking about?'

Penny flushed. 'It was a nice afternoon out,' she conceded.

The last thing Penny wanted to do was want admit to Alice that against expectations the afternoon had been a riotous success. As Roger relaxed in their company, Penny realised he had inherited Minnie's sense of fun. His wicked impersonation of the earnest hikers who strode past them had

Penny's sides aching with laughter, and it proved impossible to catch him out on Shakespeare characters when he boasted he was as knowledgeable as his grandmother.

'You've been holding out on us,' Penny had complained when yet again he had guessed the right answer.

'Minnie used to send us autographed copies of her reviews,' he admitted. 'My father was never really into that sort of thing, so I read them, then took them to school for the library to catalogue. It was a good source of income.'

'You sold your grandmother's reviews?' All Penny's good feelings towards him evaporated.

'Not for money,' Roger insisted. 'Schoolboys are always hungry, and the chief librarian used to treat us to buns and biscuits as a thank-you. I call that a good deal, don't you?'

'It's a pity you didn't see more of your grandmother when you were growing up.' Penny's words slipped out without thinking.

'I was sent to boarding school when my mother fell ill,' Roger said in a quiet voice. 'Then like I told you, we went abroad to live.'

Elizabeth chose that moment to come cycling back to the tower, her arrival creating a welcome diversion. 'I've just seen a huge seagull, and it ate one of the hiker's sandwiches. She was ever so cross. There was an awful lot of squealing.'

'From the seagull?' Roger asked.

'No, the hiker.' Elizabeth and Roger both collapsed into uncontrollable mirth. Penny cast them a despairing look.

Alice's voice broke into Penny's thoughts. 'Any more afternoons out coming up?'

'I don't know. Roger's been called up to London.'

'That's a shame. All you do is work and look after Elizabeth.'

'She's my daughter. Of course I'm going to look after her.'

'That's not what I meant. You need some down time.'

'I'm here tonight.'

'Your first night out in ages.'

'And yours.'

Alice shushed Penny. 'Lydia's coming to the end of her story; we'd better look as though we've been paying attention. She might start asking questions.'

'My turn.' Marika, elegant in a long black dress, tapped her glass and looked at everybody.

'The table's yours.' Sarah's bracelets glowed in the candle flame.

'We don't have crocodiles in Cracow,' Marika said, looking expectantly around the table. 'But we do have a dragon,' she announced with a flourish.

Katy hooted with disbelieving laughter. 'Bring it on,' Sarah invited.

'You don't believe me? For sure we do. Many years ago, our dragon terrorised everyone with his horrible flames and huge red eyes. He was covered in green scales and would roar loud and long.'

'Sounds like Miss Dottridge, our games mistress at school. Remember her?' Nicole asked Katy, who nodded in vigorous agreement.

'Then one day a brave man, his daughter's secret suitor, plucked up the courage to poison the dragon by feeding him infected meat. The king was so pleased, he allowed his daughter to marry the man she loved.' Marika finished her story to a round of applause.

'And they all live happily ever after,' Katy said with a wry twist of her mouth. 'As if.'

Penny scooped up some more of Len's aubergine bake, glad the evening was turning into such a success. The seven of them were all so very different in character, age and background, yet everyone was having a terrific time. Katy and Nicole were busy plying Sarah with questions about Australia. Marika and Lydia were vying with each other to tell the most outrageous story, leaving Penny and Alice laughing so much they were forced to wipe the tears from their eyes.

'Lydia's met her match,' Alice crowed.

'You with your stories of actors, pah.' Marika snapped her fingers. 'You have no idea how some of these supermodels behave.'

'Much like some of the stars I could name, I imagine,' Lydia replied, getting into her stride.

Marika dismissed anything so trivial with an airy wave of her hand. 'I am not talking about a star on a dressing-room door. Today's models want every luxury. They do not realise how lucky they are to have such a wonderful job. My grandparents fought hard for their family. Nothing went to waste, but that is something these girls they would not understand.'

It was Sarah who stifled the first yawn. 'I'm tuckered. In case you haven't noticed, everyone else has gone home.'

'Do you think Len would mind if we snaffled the last of the chocolates?' Nicole cast a longing glance at the foil-wrapped mints remaining on the plate.

'Leave one for me,' Alice threatened, 'otherwise I'll tell on you.'

'That's blackmail,' Katy retaliated.

A cheerful scuffle ensued as the girls fought over the heart-shaped chocolates Len had provided for them.

'When you girls finally come to order, we need to talk about transport,' Lydia announced. 'I've made arrangements for a taxi to collect me, so if anyone cares to join in . . . ? Marika, Penny, and what about Elizabeth?'

'She's doing a sleepover,' Penny said. 'I'll go up and check on her.'

'You're not staying over too?' Lydia asked.

'Bracken's booked in early tomorrow morning for a week's stay. I need to be there when he arrives.'

'The noise and the hair.' Marika shuddered. 'It gets everywhere. I hope you will not allow this Bracken into the cottage, Penny.'

'He's well behaved, really,' Penny insisted.

'That is not what Roger told me. The

dog attacked him.'

Katy leapt to Bracken's defence. 'He was only playing.'

'And they're best friends now,' Nicole insisted.

'Hey, Marika, why don't you come on one of our walks? I could show you the countryside,' Alice suggested. 'That way you'd get to like the dogs. I'm training Roger up too,' she added.

'You've done wonders with that girl,' Sarah murmured to Penny. 'We had the most amazing day out. Alice took me everywhere. You heard she's thinking of going back to college next term?'

'Yes. Len was devastated when she was forced to cut short her studies.'

'By the way,' Sarah said, opening her bag, 'I have something for you.' She passed over a small black velvet pouch. 'That brooch I mentioned — it's in there.'

'What do you want me to do with it?' Penny asked.

'The solicitor suggested I find out whether Lydia or Roger recognise it.'

'It might be valuable.'

'Perhaps you'd ask Lydia for me when you have a quiet moment?'

'If you'll excuse me,' Lydia said, pushing back her chair, 'I need to have a quick word with Len.'

'She was certainly on form tonight,' Sarah said.

'You know, she's not such a bad old thing,' Katy said as she finished off the last of the guacamole dip. 'Alice, tell Len he is the tops. Who said he couldn't cook?'

'Actually it was Lydia,' Alice confessed, biting her lip.

'You don't think . . . ' Penny was reluctant to voice her fears, but the others caught her drift.

'Perhaps we ought to go and rescue Len,' Nicole said, then jumped to her feet as Lydia re-entered the room.

'I don't want any objections . . . ' Lydia paused for full theatrical effect. ' . . . but Len and I have come to an agreement.'

'You're getting married?' Katy and

Nicole broke into a fit of the giggles.

Lydia raised her eyebrows in mock exasperation. 'What is the matter with you girls?'

'Sorry, Lids,' Nicole apologised. 'It was your delicious champagne.'

'And the canapés,' Katy added.

'Thank you very much,' the girls chorused.

Mollified by their words, Lydia flushed with pleasure, then continued. 'I have negotiated us a special rate for dinner tonight, and it's all settled.'

'I do not understand.' Marika looked puzzled. 'What have you settled? You are engaged to Len?'

'I think what our good friend Lids is saying,' Sarah explained, 'is that dinner is on her.'

'You cannot pay, Lids,' Marika protested.

Lydia dismissed her objection. 'I already have, so let's hear no more about it. Now where did I put my coat? The taxi's here and we don't want to keep him waiting. Come along, everyone.'

'Told you Lids was a good 'un,' Sarah said, nudging Penny, as everyone shuffled into the corridor.

'I feel bad about some of the things I've said about her,' Nicole admitted.

'Me too,' Katy agreed.

'Perhaps this means she's declared a truce — you know, over the Lucetta thing?'

'Now, you two girls have transport, don't you?' Lydia asked.

Katy fished her mobile phone out of her bag. 'My father said he would come and collect us.'

'Good.' Lydia began organising everyone else into some sort of order. 'Sarah and Alice, thank you for a lovely evening.' She kissed each of them on the cheek. 'In the past, when my dear Liam was alive, we would have stayed up dancing until dawn, and then we would have had breakfast on the lawn and watched the sun rise.'

Everyone listened politely with indulgent smiles on their faces. 'You haven't got any change for the taxi, have you, Marika?' Penny hissed.

'Why?'

'I thought perhaps we should pay Lydia's fare, but I don't have enough cash on me.'

'I will use my company card.'

A small blue sports car drove into the car park. 'That can't be Katy's father already,' Penny said.

'It looks like Roger Oakes to me,' Lydia said, pausing by the taxi door as the occupants of the car got out.

'You're right, it is. Darling,' Marika called over, 'how are you?' Buoyed up by champagne, she blew kisses across the car park.

'Roger, who on earth is that?' a small, dark-haired woman who was clinging to his arm demanded. 'And why is she calling you 'darling'?'

# 11

'Do you think I upset his girlfriend?' Marika was still speaking as Lydia bundled her into the waiting taxi.

'Cherry Tree Farmhouse please, driver,' Lydia called through to the front of the cab.

'Who is that woman?' Marika persisted when neither Lydia nor Penny replied. 'And why didn't they speak to us?'

'I have no idea, dear,' Lydia said, 'but it's too late to think about it now. Sit back and enjoy the ride home.'

The taxi drew out of the car park and swept down the country lane towards St Mary's. During the drive, Penny tried to convince herself that Roger's private life was none of her business. She wouldn't have minded so much if his girlfriend hadn't been so dismissive of Marika's attempts to be friendly — though Penny realised she'd reacted exactly the same way herself the first time she had met Marika, who had called Roger 'darling'. Now that Penny was better acquainted with Marika, she realised nothing was meant by it; calling people 'darling' was something artistic people did. Lydia and Minnie were often guilty of the same offence.

A wry smile curved Penny's mouth. Life in the country was proving to be more of a culture shock than she could ever have imagined. People had time for each other in St Mary's, and everyone talked to everyone else. The block of flats where she and Elizabeth had lived in London had been huge and impersonal. The residents weren't unfriendly, but their busy lives didn't leave them much time to stop for a chat. Here in St Mary's, people made the time to talk, and the sensation caused by Minnie's grandchildren turning up out of the blue had provided the neighbours with hours of happy gossip.

Penny closed her eyes and tried to follow Lydia's advice and relax. She had a full day tomorrow, starting with Bracken's arrival.

'Here we are,' Lydia announced as the taxi shuddered to a halt. 'Wake up, you two sleepy heads.'

Marika opened her bag. 'You must let me pay.'

'I wouldn't hear of it. I have an account with the taxi company. Now I no longer drive, I find it an absolute necessity. Put your wallet away.'

'The next time I will pay,' Marika promised. 'We will have another dinner out soon, yes?'

'It's a date.' Lydia patted her hand. 'I have to say, I haven't enjoyed myself so much in years. Sleep well, both of you. Now if this nice young man will give me his arm, we'll make our way across the lawn. You don't mind if I use your side gate, Penny, do you? It's so much more convenient. I hope Lucetta hasn't missed me too much. She's my pedigree Shih Tzu,' she explained to the slightly bemused driver, 'and she does fret when I go out. But I'd be lost without her.' Her voice faded away as she tottered across the lawn, clutching the driver's arm.

Marika blew Penny a kiss as she put her key in the door of the cottage. 'Good night, darling. Sweet dreams.'

Penny let herself into her flat. With her head buzzing, she knew she would find it difficult to sleep. After soaking in a long, warm bath and wrapping up in her dressing gown, she padded into the kitchen to make a milky drink. Flicking on her laptop, she cast a quick glance over her week's schedule. Every appointment was booked, and with Bracken staying over, she would have no spare time to revamp her figures. She sipped her drink, the uncertainty of her situation an ever-present black cloud.

Elizabeth had settled in well at her new school and made friends. Penny didn't want to move her. Affordable accommodation was difficult to find, especially when business accommodation was needed. Feeling more awake than ever, Penny rinsed out her mug. She had Flora Clark's telephone number on her database, but would it be fair to put her under pressure by asking if any of her contacts could help? Her nephew Sean may have only been being polite and made the gesture in an effort to ease his conscience over the bank's stance on Penny's financial affairs.

A movement outside caught Penny's attention. Flicking back the curtain, she peered down into the garden. John had mended the hencoop, but how long would his repair last? The shadows on the lawn highlighted by the waning moon were probably only the reflection of Minnie's theatrical statues, but for peace of mind Penny felt the need to make sure.

She shrugged on an old raincoat and, discarding her slippers, thrust her feet into her boots. This time she would be better prepared to confront an intruder.

She snatched up a torch, tested its beam, then rammed an old hat on her head and crept down the stairs. Grabbing her broom on the way out, she unlocked the door and peered around. As her eyes adjusted to the darkness, she could see there was no fox lurking around the wire cage of the hen house, but for no discernible reason the hairs on the back of her neck rose. Now she had grown used to the noises of the night in the country, her instinct told her she wasn't alone.

A sudden flash of light caught the corner of her eye. 'Lydia?' she called out. 'Is that you?'

There was no response. Keeping a firm grip on her torch, Penny ventured into the darkness. She heard the swish of tyres as a car drove by in the road outside. The lights faded into the distance, taking with them Penny's fears. Sagging with relief, she fumbled for the 'off' switch on her torch — then swung round at the sound of heavy breathing behind her.

'Who's there?' she called out.

'Penny . . . ' a frail voice came back at her.

'Marika? What's wrong?'

A silhouette appeared against the moonlight and collapsed into Penny's arms. The impact sent the two women staggering against the wall.

'I feel so ill.'

Penny supported Marika under her armpits and guided her towards the wooden seat.

'It's my stomach.' Marika doubled over with pain. 'I'm sorry I frighten you, but I don't know what to do.'

'I'm calling the doctor.'

'Don't leave me.' Marika grabbed Penny's sleeve. 'I don't like the dark. It scares me.'

'Can you make your way upstairs?' Penny asked.

'I don't know.'

'Try,' Penny implored. 'Let me take your weight.'

What seemed like hours later, they staggered into the kitchen. Penny stifled a cry of shock as she turned on the light. Marika was deathly white and had difficulty standing up straight. 'My stomach,' she moaned again.

'I have to get help,' Penny insisted.

A quick glance at the wall clock told her it was nearly one in the morning. She didn't know the number of an all-night doctor, and the nearest hospital was at least half an hour's drive; Penny had sipped champagne and white wine with her dinner. Inhaling deeply to calm her nerves, she dialled Lydia's number. It rang out for several minutes.

'Hello,' a sleepy voice eventually answered.

'It's Penny,' she said.

'Have I overslept or something?' Lydia mumbled.

'I'm sorry I woke you, but Marika is unwell, and I wondered if you knew an emergency call-out number,' Penny said in a rush.

A long silence followed.

'Lydia?'

'I'll be right over.'

'You don't have to come,' Penny protested, but Lydia had already hung up.

Penny dashed back to Marika's side. 'Lydia's coming to help. Everything will be fine now,' she said with a confidence she was far from feeling.

'Do not say it was her canapés that make me feel sick,' implored Marika. 'We had such a nice evening. I do not want to ruin things.'

'I had exactly the same meal as you, and I'm not feeling unwell,' Penny said. 'Would you like me to give Len a call?'

'Why?' Marika's voice came out as a gasp of pain.

'I don't know. To see if Alice or Sarah is feeling unwell?' Penny ran a hand through her hair.

'I feel hot.'

Penny put a hand on Marika's forehead. She was burning up. 'I'll get you a glass of water.'

She opened the window and let in a cold blast of evening air. Where was

Lydia? It shouldn't take this long to walk round from her cottage. A loud noise made Penny jump.

'Sorry,' came Lydia's voice. 'It's dark down here. I've walked into a broom. Hope I haven't got a black eye. Is there a light switch anywhere?' More noise followed as she stumbled around, trying to get her bearings.

'Hang on,' Penny called out. 'I've got a torch.' She clicked it on and went in search of Lydia, who, resplendent in peach silk nightwear under her dog-walking coat, was doing her best to cope with the vagaries of a garden broom and a pair of discarded boots.

'Take these,' Lydia said, thrusting the offending objects at Penny. 'Where's Marika?'

'In the kitchen.'

'Lead on up. I've brought my first-aid kit.'

'I don't think a bandage or plasters will be of much help to us.' Penny was beginning to wish she'd bitten the bullet and telephoned Roger. No doubt he'd be angry at being disturbed, but this was an emergency, and he had some responsibility for Marika. She was his sitting tenant.

'The emergency hasn't been invented that I can't cope with,' Lydia insisted. 'When you're on tour you learn to expect the unexpected. Now, Marika.' She knelt down by her chair. 'Let's see what's going on here. Stick out your tongue.'

'So sorry.' Marika broke into a stream of Polish which neither Lydia nor Penny could understand.

'We've got to get her to hospital,' Penny insisted. 'Can you ring up your taxi man?'

'He won't take her if he thinks she's going to be unwell en route. We have to think of something else. I did have an emergency number but I'm sorry, darling, I couldn't find it — and I hate to have to tell you this, but I couldn't get an ambulance either. There's been a bad road accident and all their vehicles are out on call. I have been ringing round all over the place. That's what took me so long. There, there,' Lydia soothed Marika. 'Let me put some of my eau de cologne on your forehead. It will help cool you down. Try and sip some water.'

'Stay with Marika,' Penny instructed Lydia.

'Where are you going?'

'To call Roger Oakes.'

A female voice answered Roger's mobile. 'Who is this?'

'Penny Graham. Can I speak to Roger please?'

'May I know what it's about?'

'I need to speak to Roger. Is he there?'

'He's rather busy at the moment.'

'Tell him it's to do with Marika, his tenant.'

'Is that the woman who was blowing him kisses in the car park earlier this evening?'

'Please. It's an emergency.'

'Another fox, I suppose?'

If Penny hadn't been so desperate for

help, she would have cut the call. How dare Roger discuss her with other people? She made a superhuman effort to be polite. 'Marika needs hospital treatment.'

'Then I suggest you call the emergency services. Roger can't drive her anywhere. The car he has is not insured for anything other than business purposes.' The line went dead.

'Try John Warren,' Lydia suggested, having overheard the call.

'Penny?' he answered immediately. 'Is there a problem?'

'It's Marika. She's ill and we can't get transport,' Penny began.

'Be with you in ten minutes.'

'Success.' Penny raised her fist.

Marika's head was resting on Lydia's shoulder and she was breathing deeply. 'She's still wearing her black dress,' Lydia murmured. 'Can you get her some things? They may want to keep her in. I'll stay here. If I move I'll wake her up.' She grimaced. 'Only a touch of cramp.' She rubbed her calf. 'See what you can find in the cottage.'

No longer worried about prowling foxes or other wildlife, Penny ran down the flagstone path that led to the cottage. She didn't need a torch — she would know the way blindfolded after having visited Minnie so many times during the night, usually when she had been having one of her eccentric turns, or insisting Penny join her for a nightcap because she couldn't sleep.

Marika had left the door ajar and Penny pushed it open. Negotiating half-unpacked suitcases and tea chests, she headed for the bathroom and thrust some toiletries into a sponge bag. Then, grabbing a few essentials from the bedroom, she began to make her way back down the stairs. She shrieked as a flashlight blinded her.

'Sorry, didn't mean to startle you. It's only me, Len,' a voice hissed.

'Len, what's going on?'

'I could ask you the same question,' another voice broke in.

'Roger?' Penny almost lost her

footing on the stairs.

'Len drove me over.'

Penny staggered down the last few steps and hoisted her bag over her shoulder. 'I contacted John Warren,' she said. 'Sorry you were bothered, Len.'

'What happened?' Roger asked.

Through the open door they heard a car honk its horn. 'That's John now.' Penny nudged Roger out of the way. 'Excuse me.' She ran towards the gate.

John fumbled with the latch. 'There's been an accident. I had to go round the long way. Where's Marika?'

'In the flat with Lydia. I've packed a few things.'

'Look, if I'm not needed,' Len said, 'I'll get back. I don't like to leave Alice on her own.'

'I'll stay,' Roger insisted.

'There's no need.' Penny could feel control of the situation slipping out of her grasp.

'Don't argue. Here, let me carry those for you.' Roger relieved her of her load. 'You'd better get back to Marika.'

# 12

John Warren insisted he didn't need an escort. 'I know the hospital layout like the back of my hand. I've done enough work there to find my way around without any problems.'

'My door is unlocked.' Marika clutched Penny's hand so hard she winced. 'I do not want thieves.'

'Roger's got a key,' Penny assured her gently, prising the woman's hand out of hers. 'He'll make sure your things are safe.'

John started his engine. 'Right — close the door, Penny, and we'll be off.'

Lydia was peering down the back staircase as Penny re-entered the flat. 'What's happening?' she asked.

'Len's gone home and Roger's in the cottage,' Penny told her.

'What's he doing there?'

'It is his property.'

'Not until probate is granted,' Lydia replied, a mulish tone to her voice.

'Let's not go into all that now.' Penny put a tired hand to her forehead and held open the door for Lydia, hoping she would take the hint to leave.

Lydia stood her ground. 'There's something I have to say.'

'Can it wait until morning?' Penny pleaded.

'I'd rather get it off my chest now.' Lydia tossed back her head and with a defiant look in her eyes as if inviting confrontation, and announced, 'I am dropping all charges.'

Penny blinked.

'Lucetta's paw has healed up nicely.'

Penny expelled a sigh of relief.

'It was one of my silly turns,' Lydia continued. 'I don't know what came over me.' There was a short pause before she held out a hand towards Penny. 'Am I forgiven?'

'I've already forgotten the incident,' Penny replied, and gave her a hug.

'Music to my ears.' Lydia rubbed at her nose with a tissue. 'Now ring me the moment you hear anything.' She gave Penny another quick hug before disappearing into the night.

Penny began to clear the mugs off the kitchen table. The sound of tap water gushing into the washing-up bowl drowned out the gentle tap on the door.

'Can I come in?'

Penny spun round with a start and saw Roger in the doorway.

'Sorry I abandoned you,' he continued, 'but I've been securing the farmhouse. I had no idea the locks were in such a bad way; they'll have to be replaced. I've also been having a look round. That's why I've been such a long time. The brickwork at the back of the chimney is very loose.' He frowned. 'I don't think I can allow Marika to carry on living there.' After a pause, he said, 'I know it's late, but have you time to talk?'

Penny turned off the tap. This was clearly not going to be her night for sleep. She pulled out a kitchen chair and invited Roger to sit opposite her.

'About tonight,' he began.

'I shouldn't have rung you,' Penny acknowledged.

'Yes you should,' Roger insisted.

'Your companion didn't seem to think so.'

'Hannah didn't understand the importance of your call.'

'I emphasised it was an emergency.' Penny's shoulders sagged with fatigue. 'It doesn't matter now. I don't intend to telephone you after midnight every time there's a crisis at the cottage.'

'I had Hannah's mobile and she had mine,' Roger continued with dogged determination. 'There was a mix-up. I think it must have happened when we got out of the car.'

'Well, I'm glad it's all sorted. Was there anything else?' Penny asked with a pointed look at the door.

'What's the situation with Marika?' Roger enquired.

'You know as much as I do. John's

promised to contact me the moment he has any news.'

'When Len knocked on my door and said you were in trouble . . . ' Roger began to explain.

'How did Len find out?' Penny asked.

'Lydia telephoned him. She wanted to make sure Sarah and Alice weren't feeling ill. They're fine, by the way. Anyway, Len explained the situation, then volunteered to drive me over here.'

'I hope Lydia's call didn't cause too much disruption.'

'The girls were woken up by all the noise. It was only with the greatest of difficulty that Len was able to persuade them to go back to bed. They wanted to come over to the cottage with us.'

'I'm glad you discouraged them,' Penny said with a weak smile. 'Lydia provided some canapés before dinner, and Marika thought the prawns might have disagreed with her. I knew I had to do something urgently.'

'I'm sorry I wasn't here to help.

Marika is my responsibility.'

'May I ask a question?'

'Go ahead,' Roger replied.

'I know it's none of my business, but who is Hannah?' She prompted when he didn't immediately answer her question, 'You know, your friend who answers your telephone at midnight.'

'Hannah Thomson. She's a ceramic artist. She paints surfaces. It's not something I know much about, but I've been told she's good at it. We met at a corporate buffet. I don't usually attend those sorts of parties, but this was one I couldn't get out of. Some important sponsors were there, and they asked if I would give Hannah a lift down here as she's currently without transport. As they were providing the car, I could hardly refuse.'

'She seemed to know about my last midnight call to you, when the fox almost broke into the hen house.'

'I was explaining about the wildlife in the area, and the story of the fox incident sort of slipped out.'

'Right, well thank you for telling me.'
Penny decided she was too tired to hear
any more.

'I didn't realise she had a personal
agenda,' Roger continued, 'and that she
has her eye on these premises.'

Penny was jerked awake. 'What?'

'That was rather my reaction too,'
Roger said. 'Hannah's mother lives
locally and knows all about Minnie's
theatre and what's been going on here.'

'And you've promised her the theatre
complex?'

'Of course not.'

'Perhaps you'd tell Hannah that so
far I've had no luck finding alternative
premises, but I have started making
enquiries.'

'I'll do no such thing.'

'As long as no more long-lost cousins
lay claim to the estate,' Penny continued, 'you can go ahead and sell the
cottage too once you've come to an
agreement with Lydia.'

'There's no need for anyone to do
anything at the moment. I only told you

about Hannah's intentions because I thought you ought to know.' Roger looked distinctly uncomfortable as he fiddled with a stray teaspoon that had escaped Penny's attention.

'These premises should make a very nice studio for Hannah.'

A dull flush stained the base of Roger's neck. 'This is getting us nowhere.'

The ringing of the telephone drowned out the rest of his words. Penny snatched up the receiver.

'Sorry . . . ' John's voice came faintly from the other end. ' . . . hospital.'

'I can't hear you,' Penny shouted.

'Operation.'

'What's going on?' Roger tried to grab the receiver from Penny.

'Back soon.' The line went dead.

'John?' Penny pressed the receiver several times without success. 'He's gone.'

'What was all that about an operation?'

'I don't know. If you hadn't tried to

get the receiver off me, I might have heard something. He's on his way back.'

Roger strode towards the kettle. 'In that case, we'll need something to keep us awake.'

★　★　★

Penny's second cup of coffee left a gritty taste in her mouth. 'Where can John be?'

'That's the tenth time you've looked at the clock in as many minutes,' Roger observed.

'He should have been here ages ago.'

Roger tweaked the kitchen curtain. 'The sun's about to rise. If you've nothing better to do, want to join me in watching the dawn come up? It's the best free show in the world.'

Penny crossed the kitchen and stood by his side. He opened the window a fraction, letting in the honeysuckled fragrance of the early morning air.

'Any minute now, Fire Alarm will

start up,' Penny said.

Roger turned confused blue eyes in her direction. 'You're expecting the fire alarm to go off?'

'Fire Alarm is Elizabeth's and my name for a songbird,' Penny explained with a tired smile. 'And when the mood's on him, he really lets rip.'

'Then we'd better prepare ourselves, because things are stirring.' Roger cocked an ear. 'Listen.'

The ghostly shadows behind Minnie's statues turned deep purple as the horizon softened, and a few songbirds began experimental tweets.

'When Elizabeth was a baby, we lived in a high-rise block of flats,' Penny reminisced, resting a dreamy head against Roger's solid shoulder. 'On sleepless nights I used to sit in the lounge and nurse her. Sunrises were our special time. We were so high up, the view stretched for miles across the estuary. There was a rumour you could see four counties, but I never managed to work out which ones.'

'Do you miss living in London?'

Penny shook her head. 'I thought,' she said, her voice husky from too much coffee and lack of sleep, 'I'd found the perfect place to live when I came here, but it wasn't to be.'

'You may yet be able to stay.' Roger's voice sounded as tight as Penny's.

'Don't give me false hope.' Penny stifled a yawn. 'I don't think I could deal with it.'

Roger moved in closer. Penny stiffened. Without warning the door flew open and an excited furry streak raced across the kitchen. Penny and Roger sprang apart.

Bracken's owner appeared in the doorway. 'I couldn't hold him, sorry. I know I'm early, but our flight's been rescheduled and we've got to leave for the airport right away.'

'Quiet!' Roger shouted. 'Sorry, not you,' he apologised to Bracken's master, who was still making apologetic noises. 'Sit!' he bellowed.

With his tongue lolling happily from

a corner of his mouth, Bracken obeyed the command and settled down in his favourite corner of the kitchen and promptly closed his eyes.

Bracken's owner took in Penny's and Roger's dishevelled appearances. 'I didn't wake, you did I?'

Penny flushed under his scrutiny. 'We haven't actually been to bed. What I mean is . . . ' she hastily added, casting an imploring look at Roger as she realised her words could be misinterpreted.

'Sorry, I've got to go. I'll pick Bracken up next week, if that's all right with you.'

'Now what are we going to do?' Penny asked.

'We don't have to do anything, do we?' Roger frowned.

'There'll be all sorts of rumours flying around St Mary's before lunch-time.'

'There always are.'

'About us spending the night together.'

The puzzled look on Roger's face

cleared. 'Is that all?' At that moment he looked exactly like his grandmother when something naughty had amused her.

'You don't seem to be taking the situation seriously.' Penny wished she hadn't rested her head on his shoulder. At the time it had seemed so right — but what had she been thinking of?

'I'm afraid I can only take in one drama at a time,' he said. 'At the moment we're batting way over average. I haven't room for any more.'

'You're no help at all.'

'What do you want me to do?' Roger enquired.

Bracken began to bark again. 'If you leave, he might settle.' Penny restrained the dog.

'I'm staying put until John gets back.' Again Roger looked like Minnie as he crossed his arms, with the light of battle in his eyes.

'I'm here,' another voice called up the stairs. 'I honked as I drove in, but I couldn't make myself heard above all the disturbance. Is that Bracken?'

Bracken raced to the door to greet John. 'Down, boy,' John said with a grin. He looked at Penny. 'What's this I'm hearing about you and Roger indulging in a private all-night party?'

'Never mind that now.' Penny was practically exploding with impatience. 'Marika?'

'Acute appendicitis. One of the nurses was Polish and Marika told her that she'd been having tummy trouble for a while. You should have heard them chatting away. She's scheduled to have her operation first thing in the morning.'

Bracken's body was warm against Penny's. As if sensing her need for warmth and reassurance, he didn't protest when she hugged him. He pressed his cold nose against her cheek in a gesture of solidarity. Startled, Penny laughed and let him go.

'Somebody ought to tell Lydia.' Roger stroked Bracken in an absent-minded gesture as if his thoughts were elsewhere.

'I'll put a note through her letterbox,' John said. 'I'm off home now that the excitement's over. Can I give you a lift, Roger? Or,' he added, glancing at Penny, 'are you staying on?'

'No one's staying on,' Penny insisted. 'I need to shower before Alice brings Elizabeth back and the girls arrive for the day.'

'We're being dismissed,' John said. 'Come on, Roger. I can take a hint even if you can't.'

The silence that followed their departure was only punctuated by the morning warbling of Fire Alarm.

# 13

'I've got a card from Crack Cow.' Elizabeth dashed into the day room brandishing a brightly coloured picture of the cathedral, her face alight with excitement.

Katy nudged her aside with a deft flick of her elbow. 'Careful — Dixie's feeling frisky this morning. We don't want anyone getting hurt.'

'Let's have a look, Princess.' Nicole strolled over, drying her hands on a towel. She scanned Sarah's scrawled message. 'Seems like they're having a good time sightseeing, eating beetroot soup and buying amber jewellery.'

'John must look terrific wearing amber earrings.' Katy finished her blow-dry and squeezed Dixie's ears. 'There you go, my pet. You're ready to take on the world.' The Labrador licked her fingers, its chocolate-brown eyes full of adoration.

Nicole waved Elizabeth's card in the air. 'Did you know amber is thousands of years old?'

'In that case John should feel really at home in its company.' Katy glanced over Nicole's shoulder and admired the card. 'I think I'd like to go to Cracow. All those dashing Polish men could set a girl's heart fluttering. What I wouldn't like to do with them.'

Nicole cast a warning look in Elizabeth's direction to silence Katy, but the child was playing with Dixie and appeared not to hear.

When Marika had decided to return to her home country for a short break in order to recover from her operation, Sarah had immediately suggested the two of them make a holiday of it. 'I want to see this dragon of yours,' she'd laughed, 'and you'll need an escort on the plane if you're feeling tired, so I'm your gal.'

'And I'm your man,' John Warren had insisted.

Somehow he had managed to include himself in their plans, and the three of them had flown out of Gatwick a few days earlier. According to Sarah's card, they were now enjoying their city break, with Marika acting as their guide.

Roger had visited Cherry Tree Farmhouse every day since, and Penny had heard frequent maintenance noises coming from the depths of the building. Several roof tiles had been dislodged during a week of summer storms and an upstairs window had cracked under the pressure.

Roger had also taken to joining Penny for coffee. The first time he arrived, he brought a bag of Len's special biscuits. Katy and Nicole had steadfastly refused to take a coffee break, citing the pressure of work.

'It's you he's come to see, Penny,' Katy insisted. 'Enjoy, and save the chocolate ones for me.'

Over their elevenses, Roger was more forthcoming about his background. 'My father was lost without my mother, so he took me out of boarding school. We travelled around and lived in Italy for a time. That's where I got my love of cars. We didn't return home until I was eighteen,' he explained.

'So that's why you didn't visit Minnie,' Penny sympathised.

'We couldn't afford the airfare. My father tried his hand at painting, but he wasn't a natural. He used to do odd jobs here and there, and made enough money to keep us going, but there was never much to spare. It wasn't so easy to keep in touch with home in those days, either. My Scottish grandparents were of an age that mistrusted technology. They didn't know how to email, and they weren't very good letter writers either.' Roger gave a sad smile. 'Minnie was just as bad. Every six months or so I would receive a huge envelope full of letters she had written to me. She never knew where to post them, so she'd parcel them up and wait until Dad sent her a postcard, then she'd mail them all on in one big batch.

It was difficult to read them in the right order. I was no different from most adolescent boys — I had other priorities, and reading a grandmother's letters wasn't high on my list. It's no wonder everyone lost touch with everyone else. We were scattered all over the globe.'

'I wonder why Minnie never mentioned you or Freya, or Henry.'

'Probably vanity,' Roger said. 'Actresses don't like to age.' He paused. 'My father passed away last summer, and I was making plans to stay with Minnie for a long holiday, but she was so difficult to pin down.'

'She could be forgetful at times,' Penny agreed.

'I bought her a mobile phone and keyed in my number, but she would never use it. She kept losing it, then she dropped it in a watering can and it wouldn't work anymore.'

'She always said life was too short for making plans.' Penny smiled. 'Elizabeth and I were on the spot, and she found it much easier to scuttle over with ideas for the garden or suggest an impromptu tea party. I do miss her. I suspect Lydia's lost without her too, even though they used to bicker constantly.'

'I'm glad she's dropped all charges over Lucetta. One less thing to worry about.'

Watching Roger munch on an oat and raisin biscuit, Penny remembered they were Minnie's favourites. She could almost hear her laughter in the background as she embarked on another of her outrageous stories.

'Have the solicitors made any progress with Sarah's claim?' Penny had to steel herself to ask the question, even though she was dreading the answer.

'Henry's credentials are proving difficult to authenticate. There's some confusion about his actual date of birth. Along with everything else of importance, his birth certificate seems to have disappeared.'

'And Hannah?'

'What about her?' An uneasy look

crossed Roger's face.

'Is she still interested in the theatre as a workshop for her ceramic art?'

'I haven't given her permission to go ahead with any plans, if that's what you mean.'

'I'm not too sure what I do mean.' Penny sighed.

'Lydia appears to have lost interest in her development project. And even if she doesn't pursue it, Cherry Tree Farmhouse would need a lot of attention before anyone could seriously consider making it their home.'

'Sean Turner's aunt Flora has given me one or two leads on new premises.'

'And who is Sean Turner?' Roger asked.

'My small-businesses manager.'

'The one who's been bullying you?'

Penny leapt to his defence. 'Sean isn't a bully. He's answerable to his manager and he can't make exceptions, much as he'd like to. I understand that.'

Roger looked unconvinced by her argument. 'Well, don't do anything hasty. Same time tomorrow?'

Before Penny could protest, Roger had driven off in yet another test-drive car. This one was more of the budget variety, one in which Penny couldn't imagine Hannah Thomson trying to thumb a lift.

'What's all the noise about?' Alerted by the laugher from the day room, Penny had gone in search of its source.

'Nicole says John wears amber earrings.' Elizabeth was red-faced from jumping up and down in an attempt to retrieve her postcard from Nicole, who was holding it up out of her reach.

'Tell-tale.' Nicole relented and handed Elizabeth back her card.

'I'm going to put it with my project stuff.' Elizabeth clasped her prized possession to her chest. 'Do you know when Marika's coming back, Mummy? I've got lots of questions I need to ask her. Do you think she'll write something in Polish for me? I want to get another gold star like I did with Minnie.'

'You mustn't exhaust Marika, darling,' Penny reproached her daughter. 'Remember she's convalescing.'

'She promised to help me,' Elizabeth insisted.

'I'm sure she won't break her promise. Meanwhile, why don't you practise that Polish piece on your recorder? You can play it to Marika when you next see her. I know she'd love to hear it.'

'Cool.' All thoughts of sulking, forgotten Elizabeth raced out of the room.

'I have some news,' Penny announced when things had quietened down.

Katy and Nicole immediately stopped what they were doing and looked at her with expectant eyes.

'Mrs Clark, Sean's aunt, has found us possible alternative accommodation.' Dixie whined at the mention of her mistress's name.

'Where?' Nicole asked.

'It's part of the purpose-built community complex near the new housing estate, and we're very lucky to be offered facilities. Everyone wants in.' Penny did her best to soften the blow. 'I know it hasn't got the charm of the theatre, but we can't sit around and wait for the axe to fall.'

'Can we afford it?' was Katy's blunt response.

'I've been trying to sort that one out,' Penny replied. 'Flora Clark may be able to bring some pressure to bear on the authorities.'

Katy made a noise at the back of her throat that suggested she wasn't entirely on side with Penny's optimism.

'Have you told Alice?' Nicole looked worried. 'You know how change unsettles her.'

'I thought I'd wait until things were a little more advanced,' Penny explained. 'Nothing's been agreed, and it may not be suitable for our purposes.'

'Well, I hope it isn't.' Katy's expression reflected Elizabeth's earlier pout. 'I love it here.'

'I know you do,' Penny sympathised.

'Believe me, if we had any other choice I'd leap at it.'

'We won't mention anything to Alice,' Nicole promised.

'Thanks for that,' Penny said with a smile.

Katy imparted her latest piece of gossip. 'I heard Hannah Thomson's still making a nuisance of herself. Do you know she had the nerve to visit Lydia to ask if she could rent out Liam's old studio?'

'Hope our Lids gave her a short sharp answer,' Nicole said.

'Hannah played her theatre connection card, saying her mother was in the business, but Lydia was having none of it. She told her she couldn't possibly remember everyone who crossed her path.'

'Good for her,' Nicole approved.

'That reminds me.' Penny fished Sarah's velvet pouch out of her pocket and slid the antique brooch into the palm of her hand.

'Would you look at that?' Nicole

gasped in awe as the diamond-studded ruby star winked back at her.

'That is something else,' Katy agreed.

'Where did you get it, Penny?' Nicole asked.

'Sarah gave it to me. She wondered if it had once belonged to Minnie and if Lydia would recognise it.'

'What was it doing in Australia?' Katy asked.

'Perhaps she gave it to Henry as the eldest son,' Penny suggested, 'for his wife.'

'From what Sarah told us about Henry, I'm surprised he didn't sell it,' Katy said.

'Me too,' Nicole agreed. 'It sounds as though he was always short of funds.'

'Don't you think you ought to lock it away?' Katy weighed it up in her hand. 'If it *is* valuable, we don't want it going astray.'

Penny slid the brooch back in its pouch. 'I'll put it in the safe with the accounts.'

'Well that's us done for the day.' Katy

began tidying up her workstation. 'Unless there's anything else, Penny?'

'No, that's fine. You get along. Where's Bracken?'

'Snoozing in the sunshine. Dixie's all ready to be picked up.' Dixie wagged a happy tail and smiled at everyone.

'Then off you go.' Penny shooed them out of the day room. 'Come on, Dixie, let's get a breath of fresh air before Flora arrives.'

Downstairs they found Bracken sniffing around Elizabeth's flower garden. Penny cupped her hands to her mouth to attract the dog's attention. 'Hey — out of there!' Bracken bounded over and began to chase Dixie around the hen house. 'And stop that,' Penny chided, beginning to regret having suggested an early-evening walk.

Her mobile began to vibrate in the pocket of her coat. Clipping on the leads to restrain the overexcited dogs, she answered her call. 'Penny's Parlour, Penny speaking. How may I help?'

'I need to speak to you urgently.'

Bracken tugged at his lead, almost wrenching Penny's arm out of its socket. Roger's voice faded as Penny struggled to control the lead.

'Sarah's father, Henry.'

'Sorry, I missed that.'

'The search results have come back. I wanted you to be the first to know.'

'Know what?'

'Sarah Deeds isn't Minnie's grand-daughter.'

# 14

Lydia's conservatory windows were open wide, letting in the early-evening sun. Lucetta inspected the flowerbeds, her springy tail the only visible sign of activity in the garden. A large photo album lay open on the padded cushions of a white wickerwork sofa.

'My dear Liam loved to unwind in this room,' Lydia said, 'after the stresses of the day.'

Penny insisted on returning to the matter in question — Sarah's brooch. 'How can you be sure it's fake?'

Lydia's grey eyes flickered as she refocused on Penny, sitting opposite her clutching the ruby star. She sipped some of her fruit juice before replying. 'I've handled enough stage jewellery to know coloured paste when I see it, darling. It's well done, and I'm prepared to concede the original might once have belonged to Minnie and might have been valuable. But a rare ruby star this one is not, and the diamond studs are cut glass.'

Penny tightened the drawstrings of the velvet pouch. 'Another disappointment for Sarah,' she said in a soft voice.

'That young woman has a lot to answer for.' Lydia pursed her lips.

'I thought you liked Sarah,' Penny protested.

'I did. I suppose I still do,' Lydia admitted with a show of reluctance. 'Only, I can't help thinking that her arrival on the scene has created complications. Unnecessary ones, as it turns out.'

'I don't think she intended to make a false claim.'

Lydia shook her head in a distracted manner. 'You're right, of course. Roger's the one I feel sorry for. How did he take the news?'

Penny cast her mind back to the previous Friday when he had rushed over to the theatre after his call. 'The solicitors emailed me with the news,' he had explained. 'I was in a meeting and I couldn't get back to their office before they closed for the day, but it's all here in black and white. Poor Sarah,' he added.

'He was disappointed,' Penny replied to Lydia's question.

Lydia raised her eyebrows. 'I would have thought he'd welcome the news.'

'I think he liked the idea of having Sarah as a cousin.'

'They can always keep in touch. Living halfway across the world doesn't present a problem these days.'

'Have you spoken to Sarah since she got back from Cracow?'

'Our paths haven't crossed,' Lydia replied. 'Neither have I seen Marika.' She paused. 'You've been seeing rather a lot of Roger, though, haven't you?'

Penny was annoyed to feel a blush staining her cheeks. 'He's been working on the house during his spare time.'

'When I take Lucetta out I've often seen him walking over to the theatre.'

'Cooee.' A shadow crossed the lawn. Sarah was dressed in one of her flamboyant silk creations with floaty sleeves and lots of jangly jewellery, reminding Penny of an exotic bird of paradise. 'Am I welcome?' she paused on the threshold of the French windows, a nervous smile on her face.

Lucetta trotted across the lawn and sniffed Sarah's sandals. She bent down to tweak the red bow in the dog's hair.

'Have you missed me, sweetie?'

Lucetta gave a friendly bark and began licking Sarah's toes.

'At least someone's pleased to see me.' Sarah stood up straight and looked around. 'I see John finally finished your patio, Lydia. I love your tubs of geraniums, and the wood furniture is very stylish.'

Lydia preened at the compliment, stretched out her legs and threw back her head. She was wearing tailored blue slacks and a silk shirt to match. Penny fumbled with the photo album, hoping she wasn't about to make one of her scenes. Sarah had handed her an olive branch and it would be gracious to accept the gesture.

'Thank you, Sarah. I missed not entertaining people.' Lydia's voice was warm and welcoming. 'But with my back garden resembling a builders' yard, there was nothing I could do about it. I couldn't invite anyone over, and I owe lots of people hospitality.' She paused for full theatrical effect. 'You and Penny are my first guests.'

'Then I'm honoured.' Sarah stepped forward and kissed Lydia on the cheek. 'I've brought you both an amber bracelet from Cracow.'

'How kind, and so pretty.' Lydia unwrapped her present and admired the delicacy of the stones. 'I shall wear it immediately, if you'll just help me with the clasp.'

'There you go.' Sarah stood back to admire the effect as Lydia held up her wrist.

'Marika isn't with you?' Lydia cast a glance over Sarah's shoulder.

'She's out somewhere with John.'

'Those two are getting very friendly. It must be something in the air.' Lydia cast a sly glance at Penny, whose colour hadn't quite returned to normal.

'I was the one who felt like a gooseberry on holiday,' Sarah admitted, 'but it was useful having John with us. He gets things done. What's all this?' she eyed up the albums on the sofa.

'Lydia's been looking at her old photographs,' Penny explained, 'trying to find one of your grandfather.'

'I feel such a fraud claiming Minnie was my grandmother.' Sarah gave an embarrassed smile. 'I got some shock, I can tell you, when the solicitor explained that Geoffrey Deeds, Minnie's first husband, was my grandfather, but my grandmother was his first wife, the one he married before Minnie. She was Henry's mother.'

'How were you to know otherwise?' Lydia refilled the fruit juice glasses. 'Your father wasn't around to explain the situation.'

'I really had no idea Geoffrey had a first wife, but it would explain why Roger's mother didn't mention Henry. She couldn't have been bigger than a baby when he left for Australia.'

Lydia pointed to a photo in the album next to her. It was of a theatrical line-up of actors, most of whom were dressed in costume ready to go on stage. 'That's Geoffrey Deeds, the tall man in a toga.' She leaned across and pointed to another actor in the picture. 'And if my memory serves me correctly, that lady there, the one with the flowers in her hair, was his first wife. Her name escapes me I'm afraid, but she often played Geoffrey's leading lady. I'm annoyed with myself for not remembering her earlier.'

Sarah studied the photo intently. 'Do you think she looks like me?' She showed Penny the picture.

'It's difficult to tell with all that stage make-up, but yes, I think I can see a resemblance. It's in the eyes.'

'Anyway, I'm glad it's all been

cleared up.' Lydia flicked an imaginary speck of dust off the cuff of her blouse. She was far too well-trained to allow the expression on her face to give away what she was truly feeing. 'I suppose Roger will now be able to move forward,' she said in a careful voice.

'The solicitors said I could make a claim on the estate if I wanted to,' Sarah replied. 'Roger's even suggested he make a settlement, but that's not my style.'

'What sort of settlement?' Penny queried.

'A quarter of Minnie's assets.'

'That's remarkably generous of him,' Lydia purred.

'Too right. But I said no. It was never about the money. Heck, I didn't know there *was* any. I told him his friendship was all I wanted from the estate.'

Lydia raised her hands in mock frustration. 'Minnie . . . much as I loved her, there are times when she deserved throttling. Why didn't she make things official?'

'Don't knock the old girl,' Sarah insisted. 'I wouldn't have met you lovely people if it hadn't been for her.'

'That's one way of looking at it,' Lydia acknowledged.

'Right now, as there's nothing to keep me here anymore, I suppose I'll head on back home to Oz. I don't want to outstay my welcome.'

'You haven't been able to trace any other family members in the old country?' Lydia asked.

Sarah shook her head. 'I haven't tried too hard. I'm not that much into the old days, but I hope we'll all stay friends — and if anyone fancies a holiday down under, you know where to come.'

'I've, er . . . ' Penny hesitated. ' . . . got some more disappointing news for you.'

'You're not going to tell me I'm not Geoffrey Deeds's granddaughter, are you?' Sarah smiled.

'It's about your brooch.'

'My only asset.'

'I don't know how to tell you this . . . ' Penny said.

'No worries,' Sarah insisted. 'Let me do it for you. It's fake, isn't it?'

'How did you know?' Lydia asked.

'I suspected as much. From what little I knew of my father, I worked out he wasn't sentimental. He wouldn't have cared if the thing was a family heirloom, and he was hardly going to wear it, was he? The only sensible solution would be to sell it on. And that's what he did, didn't he?'

'But why have a copy made?'

'Perhaps he did have a conscience after all,' Sarah admitted. 'Maybe he gave it to my mother and she believed it was real. Who knows?' Sarah looked at it. 'I'll keep it as a souvenir, perhaps do a little piece about its history and put it up in the shop. Visitors like that sort of thing, a historical link with home.' She slipped it back into her bag. 'I'm sorry I don't have any influence in the land development thing anymore,' she said to Penny. 'If it's any consolation, I would have voted against it, but there you go.' She shrugged, then looked at Lydia. 'How about you?'

'You mean where do I stand?'

'I guess I do.'

'I don't know. Minnie's muddled legacy was a true reflection of her life.'

'You can say that again,' Sarah replied. 'But she sounds like a fun person.'

'She knew how to work the system,' Lydia said with a wry twist to her mouth. 'She took advantage of my Liam, and with his eye for a beautiful face he was far too soft to insist on proper boundaries between our two properties. Until we get it sorted out no one will be able to make any decisions.'

'I know I don't have a say in the matter anymore, but I'd hate to see the theatre demolished,' Sarah said. 'Surely it has some heritage value.'

'Businesspeople don't see these things in the same way. As for the farmhouse, it needs a lot of work doing to it. Look what happened last night.' Lydia turned to Penny.

The previous evening they had been woken by a strong wind gusting through the trees. Bracken had been disturbed by the noise and wouldn't stop barking. Fearing another nocturnal visit from the fox, Penny raced outside, only to find Lydia in the garden inspecting the lawn, which was littered with tiles that had been blown off the roof of the farmhouse.

'It's structurally unsound,' Penny informed Sarah. 'Marika's moved out.'

'Poor kid. She's having a tough time of things, what with losing her first place, then falling ill. Where's she going to live now?'

'She can stay with me.' Lydia snapped shut her photo album.

'Hey, that's a great idea.' Sarah beamed at her.

'I've plenty of room, and Lucetta adores her — don't you, my pet?'

'What about Hannah Thomson?' Penny feigned ignorance on the supposedly spirited exchange the two of them had had. 'Doesn't she have first call on Liam's studio?'

'I'm fussy who I share my home with, and I do not choose to offer accommodation to that young lady. Did you know her mother had the nerve to ring me and claim she'd advised me on my wardrobe during my Australian tour?'

'I'm guessing she didn't,' Sarah said.

'My dresser had sole responsibility for my costumes on that tour. I happen to remember she was a lovely lady from Perth who knew exactly how to deal with the vagaries of the Antipodean climate. When I mentioned this fact, Hannah's mother suggested she might have been mistaken and we might have worked together in Manchester.'

'Perth, Australia; Manchester, England — easily confused.' Sarah was now openly laughing.

'Not in *my* head.' Lydia was in full flow. 'Can you believe the next day Hannah was knocking on my door, saying her mother had arranged everything and when could she move in? I told her I had made other arrangements, and I have — now. Marika can have the rooms.'

'In that case,' Sarah whipped out her mobile phone, 'before you change your mind, I'm sending her a text.'

'You do that,' Lydia replied with a firm nod of her head.

'Then how about we have that girls' night out I promised us before I disappear back to Australia?'

'Let's dress up. Do things in style,' Lydia suggested.

'Good idea, Lids. I could wear my ruby brooch.'

'I suppose it won't do any good reminding you my name is Lydia?' she asked, trying to look annoyed.

'None at all.' Sarah winked at Penny and began tapping in her text.

# 15

'Hello there,' Lydia, resplendent in a crushed raspberry shirtwaist dress, greeted Roger in the car park of The King's Head.

Roger looked up, red-faced from struggling to get his briefcase out of the back seat of a family saloon.

Sarah, equally stunning in a turquoise caftan, sauntered towards him. 'Why don't you pull it through the sun roof, sweetie?'

'Because I am road testing its practicality for the rigours of everyday life.'

Penny joined the small group. 'He's working,' she explained to Sarah, who was looking at him with a bemused expression on her face.

'Right,' she responded.

Roger opened his mouth to speak but Sarah got in first.

'Well, it's up to you, Rog, of course. But if you'll let me show you how . . . ' She leaned over and grabbed at the leather bag. 'And there you have it.' She deposited the briefcase at his feet. 'That's how you successfully navigate baby seats and shopping bags.'

'For someone who doesn't have children,' Lydia drawled, 'you're remarkably adept at dealing with family life.'

'In my time, Lids, I've done all sorts of jobs, including being a nanny to a toddler with an acute case of the terrible twos.'

Lydia shuddered. 'Not my scene at all.'

Sarah put an arm around Lydia's shoulders and laughed. 'Nothing would faze you, Lids. You're far too much of an old pro.'

'Is that a compliment?' Lydia asked.

'It is indeed. It means respect.'

Sarah and Penny laughed at her confusion, then high-fived.

'For heaven's sake,' Lydia tutted.

'We're having a good time,' Sarah insisted.

'In the car park of The King's Head?' Lydia curled her lip. 'I can think of better places.'

'Lighten up, Lids.'

'Lydia's right, you know.' Roger locked the car door.

'About what?' Penny asked.

Sarah supplied the answer. 'I think what Rog means is, why am I so happy when I've been proved a fraud?'

'Hang on,' Roger said, grabbing Sarah's arm. 'I didn't mean that.'

'I know exactly what you meant, Rog, and if you weren't such a nice guy I'd have taken it the wrong way.'

'I never said you were a fraud, did I?' he asked with a perplexed frown.

'I lost out, but it's cool, I can handle it. So if it's been playing on your mind — chill. We're all friends here, aren't we?'

Lydia took charge of the situation. 'Come on, everyone. Len's booked us

227

the table in the window so we can look out onto the garden. And I don't know about you, but I am famished.'

'Lids, help me rustle up the gang.' Sarah linked arms with Lydia and, with a telling look over her shoulder and a whispered aside to 'stay where you are' to Penny, guided Lydia inside.

'What was all that about?' Roger asked when he and Penny were alone.

'I think it's Sarah's way of saying if we want a quiet word, she'll make sure we're not interrupted.'

'That lady can read minds.' Roger ruffled his hair. 'I've been talking to Hannah and I wanted to tell you about it,' he admitted.

'Oh yes?' Penny raised an eyebrow.

'She says you've registered interest in an industrial unit.'

'How does she know?' Penny asked.

'Apparently she had her eye on it.'

'Then you can tell her she's wrong. Flora Clark was making enquiries on my behalf and she told me there was a unit available. I was going to drive over and inspect it the other day but I got held up.'

'In that case I'm available.'

'To do what?'

'Run you over to the unit.'

'When?'

'How about tomorrow? And don't tell me you're busy. It's Sunday. Your parlour is closed.'

'Will the unit be open for inspection on a Sunday?'

'It's their busiest day for viewings, from what I've heard.'

'And you can't wait to fix me up?' Penny hadn't meant her words to sound so bitter. 'I've told you, Roger, I'll leave as soon as I can.'

'Why do you and Sarah insist on taking everything I say the wrong way?' he asked.

'Time's up,' Alice bellowed from the dining room window. 'Marika's arrived, and she's full of tales of Renaissance architecture and Gothic towers. You should hear what she and John got up to at the artisan cheese festival. Sarah says to tell you that Katy and Nicole are on their way, and there's chilled white wine all ready for you on the table.'

'What's going on?' Roger asked, casting his eyes up and down Penny's dress. 'Why are you all dressed up to the nines?'

'Girls' night out,' Penny replied. 'Marika and I raided her autumn collection box. This I'll have you know is next season's colour.' She did a twirl for his benefit.

'I like it,' Roger said in a voice warm with approval.

'Penny,' Alice said as she poked her head out of the window, 'I shan't tell you again.'

'I think you'd better join them,' Roger said with a laugh.

Penny wished his smile didn't make her fingertips tingle quite so enthusiastically. Her emotional skills were too rusty to deal with the rigours of a relationship. Whilst she hadn't closed her mind to ever starting another one, since she had become a single parent and moved to St Mary's her life had lurched from one crisis to another. There hadn't been time to think about relationships.

And that was why she hadn't seen this one coming. She had been caught unawares, and was now in danger of entertaining deep feelings for Roger Oakes, a man who was about as far from her idea of a life companion as she could imagine. Who in his or her right mind could possibly consider falling for someone who had the power to evict them?

Unaware of the effect just looking at him was having on Penny, Roger firmed up their arrangements. 'I'll pick you up tomorrow. Ten o'clock?'

★　★　★

'I'll look after Elizabeth for you,' Lydia insisted in the taxi on the drive home. 'We'll have a day in the garden before the weather breaks. She can help me with my new bedding plants. If we run

231

out of things to plant, then she can work on her project with Marika. You go and enjoy yourself.'

'It won't be a fun day,' Penny insisted. 'I need to inspect these new premises Mrs Clark has found for us.'

'Call it what you like, darling, but do it. Sleep tight.'

*   *   *

The next morning Penny chose comfortable Capri pants and a sweatshirt emblazoned with the pet parlour's logo. Roger drove up at ten o'clock on the dot.

'Thought I'd put this one through its paces.' He indicated the family saloon that had caused him grief the previous evening. 'We could go for a drive out into the country afterwards. Sorry I can't offer the sporty Italian number I had last week, but the job isn't all about glamour.' He started up the engine. 'You OK with the sunroof open? I have to test everything. Hope it closes efficiently.' He cast an anxious glance at the louring clouds.

Penny's heart sank as she eyed the modern complex, a structure that housed a fitness block, leisure facilities and several industrial units. Then she cast an eye down the list of the businesses already occupying the premises. Most seemed to be involved in modern technology. She doubted they would welcome an influx of overexcited dogs.

'Do you know the number of your unit?' Roger asked.

'Thirty-six,' Penny replied with a lack of enthusiasm.

Roger drew up outside the sales office. Penny shuddered. 'Awful thought, isn't it — the idea of a row of corporate flags flapping over Cherry Tree Farmhouse,' he said, as if reading her mind. 'Still, now we're here we'd better go through with it.'

'What do you think?' Penny tried to look out of the small window at the back of the north-facing unit, but it was too small and too high.

'Honest opinion?' Roger asked. Penny nodded. 'I hate it, but I don't have to like it. It's your decision.'

'Mrs Clark has been so kind. How can I disappoint her? I need daylight and grounds to exercise the dogs. The only fresh air we would get would be through that tiny window and I couldn't let any of the dogs loose. It wouldn't be safe.'

'Hello,' came a familiar male voice from behind.

'John?' Penny spun on her heel. 'What are you doing here?'

'Last-minute maintenance work. You're not thinking of moving in, are you?' he asked with a concerned frown. 'Because if you are, a word of warning . . . ' He looked over his shoulder as if to ensure they wouldn't be overheard. 'I'd think twice if I were you.'

'Why?'

'There are all sorts of things you can and can't do under the terms of the lease.'

'Such as?'

'No late-night working, special rates for running water, the electricity bills are high, and you can't have access over the weekend.'

'What?'

'The word on the street is strictly nine to five, five days a week, with no exceptions.'

'It's Sunday today and the sales office is open.'

'Do you see anyone else around apart from potential customers?'

Penny peered out of the door. The area was deserted.

'That settles it,' Roger said. 'You can't come here.'

'It's my decision,' Penny insisted.

'If you want my opinion,' John said, 'I agree with Roger. These premises aren't right for you.'

'Then what am I going to do?'

'Things usually sort themselves out, my old nan used to say, and she was never wrong,' John assured her.

'I know you're trying to be kind,

John.' Penny managed a shaky smile. 'But to quote *my* grandmother, fine words don't butter any parsnips.'

'You know, I never could work out exactly what that saying meant,' John responded. 'Anyway, I'm glad I bumped into you. Marika's moving in with Lydia today, isn't she?'

Penny glanced at her watch. 'I should be getting back. I promised to help with her boxes.'

'There's no rush. Enjoy your day in the countryside. I'll look after Marika.'

'Let's go for that spin I promised you,' Roger said as he locked up the unit. 'You can help me review the car. That way I'll be able to treat you to lunch on expenses.'

They stopped by a running water mill that boasted a small restaurant round the back. Roger ordered two homemade fruit juices. 'What would you like to eat?'

They opted for the house special salads, then found seats in the conservatory. It overlooked the stream, and ducks paddled enthusiastically in the water while children played on the grass.

'Idyllic scene, isn't it?' Penny leaned back in her padded garden seat.

One of the ducks waddling a little too fast wound up taking an undignified tumble, its orange webbed feet flapping in the air, followed by outrageous quacking.

'Know how the poor chap feels,' Roger sympathised. 'I always seem to fall flat on my back too.'

'I don't follow.'

'Everyone adored Minnie. I'm not so good at people skills.'

'I wouldn't say that,' Penny insisted. 'You're different in character, that's all, and Minnie was unique.'

'Even so, the last few weeks haven't been easy.'

'What are you going to do now that Sarah's . . . out of the picture?'

'We need to get Lydia's boundaries sorted out. Her husband was as bad as Minnie when it came to dealing with officialdom. No one bothered to write anything down or discuss the details.'

'Have you heard about Sarah's brooch?'

'That it's a fake?' Roger nodded. 'Sometimes this whole situation doesn't seem real.'

The waitress interrupted them with their order, and they tucked into their plates of prawns and crusty brown bread. 'I haven't eaten a meal this good for ages,' Penny said as she mopped up the last of her prawn sauce with her bread.

'Can you manage some strawberries for dessert?'

'I shouldn't.'

'Let's share a dish,' Roger suggested, and Penny relented. Soon they were enjoying a delicious bowlful, with a dollop of cream.

'Now I really can't manage another mouthful,' she insisted as she scraped some cream off the bowl with her spoon.

'This is what Sundays should be

about,' Roger said. 'Lazy lunches, laughing at ducks and enjoying the sunshine.'

In the distance they heard the distant but unmistakeable rumble of thunder. Roger pulled a face. 'You'd better hope I was only joking about not being able to close the sun roof,' he said.

By the time they reached the car, fat blobs of rain were bouncing off the cobblestones. Anxious parents gathered up their children. The ducks paddled for cover.

The wipers swept across the windscreen as Roger started the engine, and the tyres swished through the puddles along roads darkened by the storm's jagged shadows. Lightning crackled through the sky, pursued by angry growls of thunder.

'Thank goodness Marika's moved out.' Roger drew up in the lane outside Cherry Tree Farmhouse. 'If it carries on raining like this, I don't hold out much hope for the roof. I'd best get back to The King's Head as soon as possible.'

'I'll be in touch,' Penny called out, skilfully avoiding a deep puddle as she jumped from the car and ran through the storm towards the blurred lights of Lydia's cottage.

# 16

Elizabeth had her nose pressed up against Lydia's conservatory window. 'Mummy!' she shouted as she waved enthusiastically. 'It's raining.'

Lydia flung open the door. 'Come in quickly and dry off.' She ushered Penny inside and thrust warm towels into her hands. 'We've been looking out for you.'

Marika, in a stylish work shirt and tailored jeans, greeted Penny with a kiss. She had fastened her hair into a topknot that had become loose, but even the stray tendrils of hair managed to look elegant. Life could be so unfair, Penny thought. Marika would look stunning wearing a bin liner.

'I had an umbrella ready, but in all the rain we did not see you,' Marika said.

'We've been ever so busy,' Elizabeth announced. 'John's been here. He helped Marika move her stuff, and Lydia let me play with her feathery thing.'

'It's called a boa,' Lydia said with a distracted air. 'You know, this looks serious.' She nodded towards the window. In the distance lightning split the sky. 'Where's Roger?' She had to shout above the overhead thunder.

Penny shook raindrops out of her hair. 'He's driving straight back to The King's Head. He didn't want anything to happen to the car he was test-driving.'

'Have some supper with us, and if the weather's no better I suggest you spend the night here,' Lydia offered.

'The theatre's only on the other side of the hedge,' Penny protested.

'Stay,' Marika chimed in. 'I will treat you to some wild mushroom soup, served Polish style with pasta and made to my grandmother's recipe.'

'Sounds an excellent idea,' Lydia agreed, 'and just the night for soup. Look at it out there. What does the weather think it's doing? No one would ever believe it was the middle of summer.'

'Perhaps it'll pass soon,' Penny said as she finished drying her hair with the towel Lydia had provided.

'I'm not so sure.' Lydia was still frowning.

'Let's go into the kitchen,' Marika suggested. 'We can talk while I stir the soup.'

'I'll turn the heating up a notch,' Lydia said. 'We don't want anyone catching a summer cold.'

'This is not cold,' Marika insisted with a laugh, 'and you should see some of the storms we have in my home town.'

'You didn't have to bring one back with you.' Lydia turned the thermostat dial.

'Is that why you're moving to Australia?' Elizabeth asked, then with a gasp put an anxious hand to her mouth. 'I wasn't supposed to say anything, was I?'

Lydia almost dropped the soup bowls she was carrying. 'What's all this?'

Marika's face turned as red as the beetroot salad she was making to go with the soup. 'I was going to tell you all over dinner,' she began to explain. 'That's one of the reasons I wanted you to stay, Penny. John has promised to join us later. He was going to bring Sarah with him, but I think perhaps they have been delayed by the bad weather.'

Lydia was the first to recover her composure. She continued setting the table. 'I think this calls for a glass of wine and some juice for Elizabeth.'

Penny wished she could open a window, but the rain wasn't letting up. 'Is there anything I can do to help?' she asked.

'Taste this.' Lydia thrust a glass of white wine into her fingers. 'Is it cool enough?'

'Lovely.'

'Would you like some water too?' Lydia asked. 'Your colour's rather high.

We don't want you catching a fever.'

'I'll sort it.' Pleased to have something to do, Penny joined in the general activity.

Without warning, Marika shrieked.

'Good grief, Marika, what's wrong?' Lydia stalled, wine bottle in hand. 'I nearly poured wine all over the table.'

'There's a face at the window.'

They all followed the direction of her shaking finger.

'Well, I'm pretty certain it's not Charles the cavalier. He'd probably get his fancy hat wet in this weather,' Penny said with a laugh.

'Will you stop it?' Lydia chided, and bustled across the kitchen to open the back door.

Two new arrivals squelched through into the kitchen, leaving large puddles on the floor. 'It wasn't raining this hard when we left The King's Head.' John was doing his best to wring the drips out of the bottom of his work trousers.

'Hi, sweeties.' Sarah blew everyone a

kiss. 'Is it all right to come in?'

Lydia took charge of the situation. 'It looks like you already have. Hang your coats over there by the Aga. Lucetta, move yourself.' She nudged the dog with the toe of her elegant shoe. 'You're in the way.'

Casting a less than loving glance in her mistress's direction, Lucetta reluctantly got to her feet and proceeded to make a dignified exit into the living room.

'She does love to sulk,' Lydia laughed. 'Now, wine? Or would you prefer a beer, John? You are staying for dinner? Marika's doing us Polish mushroom soup with wheat rolls.'

'And cinnamon apples to follow,' Marika chimed in.

Sarah held up a bag of Len's scones. 'We haven't come empty-handed.'

Lydia retrieved two more bowls from the cupboard and began searching around for extra cutlery. 'I would suggest we eat in the conservatory, but I don't think watching the storm would be very pleasant. So if no one minds squashing up, I'm sure we can all manage in here.'

The kitchen was redolent with the smell of simmering soup and the spicy cinnamon of Marika's apples. 'All ready,' she announced.

Sarah stood next to her. 'I'll provide the bowls if you provide the soup. That smells fantastic.'

With much scraping of chairs, everyone sat down. Bread began to be passed up and down the table.

Elizabeth's lower lip wobbled as she ignored her bowl of soup. 'I'm sorry, I forgot it was a secret,' she told John.

Sarah leaned forward a conspiratorial smile on her face. 'You let the cat out of the bag?'

Tears threatened to well up in Elizabeth's eyes. 'Sorry,' she repeated in a whisper, and lowered her head.

'No, it's great,' Sarah said, stroking her head. 'Saved us the bother of explanations.'

'Then it's true?' Lydia asked in a

faint voice. 'You're going to Australia, Marika?'

'When did you decide all this?' Penny asked in almost as faint a voice.

'One at a time, please.' Lydia raised a hand as three anxious voices did their best to bring her and Penny up to speed.

'You first.' Sarah nodded at Marika.

'I think perhaps the soup won't wait.' She inspected the contents of her bowl.

'Suits me.' John picked up his spoon. 'I am famished. I wouldn't have volunteered for the job if I'd have known moving you in here would be such tough work.'

'You'll have to man up if you want to prove yourself down under,' Sarah warned him.

'Everyone has enough?' Marika checked out the table.

'Manners be blowed,' Sarah said. 'I'm going to tear into this lovely bread with my fingers and use it to soak up the mushrooms.'

For several moments no one spoke.

Eventually spoons scraped the empty bowls against a background of wailing wind and distant rolls of thunder.

'Let's hope we've heard the last of that box of tricks,' John remarked as the storm began to move on. 'Did I mention the lane's flooded? We had to take the long way round. That's why we were late.'

'You didn't pass Roger, did you?' Penny asked with a twinge of alarm.

'We couldn't see much at all,' John admitted. 'Even with the wipers on double speed, we were finding it difficult to cope.'

'I don't think we saw anyone,' Sarah added, 'but you'd have to be desperate to go out on a night like this.'

'I'm sure Roger will be fine,' Lydia reassured Penny. 'He's tough. He comes from Scotland, remember. Anyway, to go global . . . Australia?' Lydia asked.

'I don't really know how it happened,' Sarah admitted. 'One evening we were in this lovely cellar restaurant in Cracow, and I said it was time I thought about going home.'

'I said I'd always fancied the idea of going to Australia,' John put in. 'And Marika said she would like to go too, because it's a nice warm country, and somehow we decided on going as a threesome.'

'It was my country working its magic,' Marika said.

'In that case we should have all ended up in Cracow,' John pointed out.

Glad she was no longer the centre of attention, Elizabeth began to fidget. 'Please may I go and play with Lucetta?' she asked Penny in a plaintive voice. 'I've finished my soup.'

'As long as Lydia doesn't think you're being impolite,' Penny insisted. 'She is our hostess.'

'Of course I don't mind.' Lydia smiled. 'Grown-up talk can be boring. Off you go. Lucetta will be glad of the company. I expect she's finished sulking by now.'

'Why don't you take some apple pie

with you?' Marika suggested.

'But don't give any to Lucetta,' Lydia said. 'I've taken Sarah's advice and put her on a diet.'

'Good on you,' Sarah approved as Elizabeth disappeared into the lounge, carefully clutching a portion of apple pie.

'Elizabeth, she did not tell you everything.' Marika was still rather red in the face.

With a smile, John leaned across the table and clutched her hand. Sarah beamed at the pair of them.

'We would like to get married,' Marika said in a rush.

'Yup, we're engaged,' John confirmed.

Lydia clapped her hands together in delight. 'Really?'

'No kidding,' Sarah insisted. 'I watched him go down on one knee and propose.'

'That's wonderful news,' Penny joined in the congratulations.

'Not sure my knees agree with you,'

John admitted with a shamefaced smile. 'It was only when I got down there that I realised the floor was solid stone, hard and cold.'

'Are you actually emigrating to Australia?' Penny asked.

'If they'll have us,' John replied.

'But what about Marika's Moderns and all your lovely new collection of clothes?'

'Hey,' Sarah rebuked Penny, 'we're a pretty cosmopolitan lot where I come from. She can re-open in Sydney, no worries. I know everyone will adore her.'

'And me too, I hope,' John said.

'You'd land on your feet anywhere,' was Lydia's crisp response.

Penny smiled at the happy couple. 'I couldn't be more pleased for you, even if it has come as something of a shock.'

'Now all we need to do is get you and Rog sorted out,' Sarah said. 'I've discovered I'm pretty good at this sort of thing. Leave it to me.'

Penny opened her mouth, but before

she could protest there was a ground-shaking thud. 'Elizabeth!' She was on her feet in a second.

'I'm OK, Mummy.' Her daughter raced back into the kitchen with a furiously barking Lucetta at her heels. 'But I saw something fall off Minnie's cottage and land on the lawn.'

Everyone scrambled to look out of the window. 'What on earth's happened?' Penny struggled to see into the darkness.

Lydia, who was standing behind her, craned her neck to see over the group now clustered by the door. 'I think the storm's got the better of Cherry Tree Farmhouse. It looks as if the something that's fallen off Minnie's roof is her chimney.'

A flash of lightning zigzagged across the lawn. 'There's someone in the garden!' Sarah shouted.

'Have they been flattened by the chimney?' Marika shrieked.

'No, they haven't,' John said, doing his best to inject some calm into the situation. 'Whoever it is, they aren't flat on their back — they're sprinting towards us.'

'Quick, Sarah, let him in,' Penny urged. 'It's Roger.'

'What's he doing running around my lawn in the middle of a storm?' Lydia asked.

'I couldn't get through. Floods,' Roger gasped, falling through the doorway. 'I turned back. I was in the cottage, and . . .' He gasped, unable to go on.

'Get him a seat, someone,' Lydia called out, 'before he collapses on the floor.'

'Are you hurt?' Penny put a hand on his chest, sick at the thought of him being injured. She could feel his heartbeat against her fingers.

'I'm all right,' he insisted.

'Here you are, mate.' John nudged a chair under the back of his legs.

'Thank you.'

He threw back his head, causing an alarmed Penny to gasp, 'There's a gash on your forehead.'

'I blundered into something in the darkness,' he explained with a weak smile.

'Well, there's nothing we can do about anything now,' Sarah said. 'I suggest we get Rog cleaned up, then try to get back to The King's Head.'

'I wouldn't hear of it,' Lydia insisted. 'I've plenty of blankets, and enough food in the freezer to see us through a siege. You're all spending the night here.'

'Elizabeth and I can easily make our way back to the theatre,' Penny said. 'The storm's abating.'

'With bits of Cherry Tree Farmhouse flying about the place?' Lydia scoffed. 'Not a good idea. I suggest we wait until morning to see the extent of the damage.'

'I'd better contact Len,' Sarah said. 'He'll be worried about us. Then why don't we leave Penny to attend to Rog's wounds?'

When John looked about to interrupt, she calmly shoved him in the back. 'Hey, stop that,' he protested.

'Come along, John.' Marika linked her arm through his. 'We will enjoy the last of the wine in the living room while we make plans for the future.'

'Yes, dear,' he answered with an impish smile. 'Honestly, I'm having second thoughts about this marriage lark,' he protested.

'Marriage?' Roger frowned.

'He and Marika are engaged,' Penny said.

'Here you are.' Lydia produced cotton wool and a bottle of antiseptic. 'If you need any help, we're in the living room.' With a telling look at Penny, she closed the kitchen door carefully behind her.

# 17

'That stings like mad.' Roger jerked his head away from Penny's ministrations.

'Man up.'

'I beg your pardon?'

'It's one of Sarah's expressions.'

'I'll see to it,' Roger insisted, snatching the bottle and cotton wool out of Penny's hands. 'What can I smell?' He wrinkled his nose.

'Mushroom soup and apple pie.'

'Any left over?' He inspected his reflection in the mirror and dabbed at his wound. 'Seafood salad is nice, but I ate mine hours ago.'

'Here you are.' Penny placed a bowl of soup on the table and cut a hunk of bread. 'You frightened the life out of Marika. She thought you were Charles the cavalier.'

'I don't feel much like a cavalier at the moment.' He began tucking into his supper. 'Did I miss something earlier?' he asked. 'John and Marika?'

'They're engaged. Sarah's been matchmaking.'

'When did all this happen?'

'In Cracow.' Penny couldn't resist adding, 'She thinks we'd be a good match too.'

Roger paused, his soup spoon half-way to his mouth.

'There's no need to look so stunned,' Penny insisted.

'Isn't there?' Roger returned his attention to his soup.

'I can't help thinking Minnie would have liked the idea.'

'As I've said before, my grandmother had some very strange ideas.'

'You think I'm strange?' Penny put her hands on her hips and leaned back in her chair.

'That isn't what I meant.' Roger's frown turned into a smile. 'You're at it again, aren't you? Teasing me.'

'You're an irresistible target,' Penny admitted, wishing his unkempt hair didn't look quite so attractive. In the warmth of the kitchen it had gone soft and wavy, and the makeshift bandage he'd stuck over his wound gave him a slightly rakish air — rather like a latter-day cavalier, Penny couldn't help thinking. 'Would you like some apple pie?'

'Thank you.' Roger poured out a glass of wine in a distracted manner. 'Actually,' he began slowly, 'you're right. It might not be such a strange idea.'

Penny refilled her own glass and took an unladylike slurp to steady her nerves. 'What might not be such a strange idea?' she asked carefully.

His complexion now resembled that of Marika's when she had been cutting up the beetroot salad. 'Minnie wouldn't have wanted the theatre to be demolished, and at the moment it's the only structurally sound part of the estate,' he battled on. 'We could come to an arrangement.'

'Let me get this right.' Penny decided

it had to be the overhead lighting turning Roger's eyes such a deep shade of blue. Everything about him seemed more defined in the warmth of Lydia's kitchen. 'If I want to stay on, you're part of the bargain?'

'I wouldn't put it quite like that.'

'Wouldn't you?'

'No.'

'How would you put it then?' She couldn't help feeling sorry for Roger. He wrote excellent motoring reviews, but when it came to the spoken word there was room for development.

'I've been offered a permanent post working for a local publisher,' he ploughed on, getting redder by the second. 'And I thought if I moved to St Mary's on a permanent basis, we could look into the idea of establishing a community centre.'

'We could?'

'You're already running a pat-a-dog scheme. We could develop things.'

'What about Lydia?' Penny asked.

'You mean you're up for it?'

'I didn't say that, but keep your voice down.'

'Why?'

'I wouldn't put it past Lydia to be listening at the keyhole.'

Roger looked shocked. 'Surely not.'

'You'd better believe it. They're all as high as kites because Marika and John are engaged.'

'I know that. You just told me.'

'What I didn't add was that they're planning to move to Australia with Sarah.'

'They are?' Penny nodded. 'Then John Warren won't be calling round here every five minutes?'

'Not from Australia, no.' Penny's lips curled with amusement. 'Are you jealous?'

Roger frowned. 'No. Anyway, he's engaged to Marika.'

'Exactly.'

They lapsed into silence.

'Where were we?' Roger eventually asked after he finished smiling at Penny.

'Are you having difficulty keeping

up?' she responded.

'I'm beginning to think that crack on my head has addled my brain. I'm not sure what's going on.'

'We were talking about a business partnership,' Penny clarified. 'I can't speak for the others.'

'That's right, a community centre. But we would need Lydia to fall in with our plans.'

'Not so fast,' Penny insisted. 'I haven't agreed to anything. And you haven't mentioned Hannah. Where does she figure in all this?'

'She's given up on the idea of having a studio down here. The locals haven't taken to her and she's done nothing to fit in with the community. She's moving back to London; much more her scene.'

Penny glanced out of the window. A weak sun was breaking through the clouds.

'Do fancy a breath of fresh air?' Roger asked.

'You're not suggesting a walk, are you?'

'The storm's passed over and I've got a couple of hard hats in the car. We could inspect the damage to the farmhouse.'

Glad to be on safer ground, Penny screwed the top back on Lydia's bottle of antiseptic. 'I'll borrow one of Lydia's waterproofs.'

Their shoes sunk into the grass as they skirted the distressed chimney-stack embedded in the lawn. 'Steady how you go.' Roger's fingers were warm as he intertwined them with Penny's. The air smelt of damp leaves and soggy mud, and a cool breeze blew in from the west.

'How did that happen?' It was all Penny could do not to shriek at the gaping hole in the roof where the chimneystack should have been.

'I'm not sure. Have you got any more suitable footwear?' Roger looked down at Penny's summer shoes.

'Minnie always kept several pairs of boots in the outhouse. I'll see what I can find.'

She trudged back in a sturdy pair of Wellingtons. 'These will have to do.'

Roger crammed one of the hard hats on her head. 'Come on then, and take care.'

Penny wrinkled her nose as she looked at what remained of the sitting room. 'It's a mess.'

He ran a finger over the back of a chair. 'There's soot everywhere.'

They advanced slowly into the room. 'What's that?' Penny nudged a sealed tin box with the tip of her boot.

'I've no idea. I've never seen it before.' Roger stooped down, picked it up and shook it. 'It's not very heavy.'

'I suppose it's locked.'

'You suppose right.'

John poked his head through the open doorway. 'Need any help?'

'Can you open this?' Penny pointed to the tin box.

John took it out of her hands and inspected it. 'It shouldn't present too much of a problem. I'll get some tools out of my van.'

Lydia's eyes were bright with anticipation as everyone gathered round the kitchen table. 'Isn't it exciting? I'll put an old cloth on the table so the tin doesn't make a mess.'

Sarah ran her hand over the dented lid. 'It's taken a few knocks in its time.'

'I wonder where it had been hiding,' Lydia said.

'In my home town, people would bury valuables in secret places,' Marika explained, 'if they didn't want the authorities to get hold of them.'

'Did Minnie have any valuables?' Penny asked Roger.

'She sold everything off to finance the theatre,' Lydia replied.

John struggled into the kitchen, clutching his toolbox. He flipped open the lid. 'I'm sure there'll be something in here that will do the trick.' He produced a selection of keys on a ring.

'You're not going to break in?' Marika grabbed his arm.

'Roger?' John looked at him.

'It's fine with me.'

'This key looks as though it might fit.'

'Have you done this sort of thing often?' Sarah asked.

'From time to time people need keys for a variety of reasons, and over the years I've sort of built up a selection. Now — quiet, everyone. I need to concentrate.'

They all held their breath as John turned the key. There was the faintest of clicks. 'We have lift-off,' he said. 'Over to you, Roger.'

'Steady on, Marika.' Sarah eased her hand out of the woman's clutches. 'I'm sure it's not full of Sydney funnel-webs.'

'There might be one or two St Mary's funnel-webs though,' John joked, wiping cobwebs off his fingers.

'What on earth do you think Minnie was playing at if she was hiding this away?' Roger said, looking puzzled.

'She so loved a drama,' Lydia said.

Everyone fell silent again as Roger carefully opened the lid and looked inside. He said nothing.

'Don't keep us in suspense,' Penny pleaded.

'Have you found anything?' Sarah asked.

'Yes.'

'Then what is it?' Lydia now joined in.

'An envelope.'

'Is that all?' Sarah looked disappointed.

'Knowing Minnie, it's probably stuffed full of unpaid bills,' Lydia commented.

'Is there any writing on the envelope?' Penny asked.

'Yes.'

'You know, Rog, if you aren't a little more forthcoming in the next ten seconds I may hit you over the head with Marika's soup ladle,' Sarah threatened.

'It's addressed to me,' Roger replied.

'Then open it.'

'And Penny.'

'Me?' Penny choked.

'Give the darned thing here.' Sarah snatched it out of Roger's hands. 'If he won't open it, will you?' she said, looking at Penny.

'I don't know that I should.'

John closed up his toolbox. 'Well, I'm done. I expect the flooding will have gone down now, so do you want a lift back to The King's Head, Sarah?'

'You can stay over if you like,' Lydia cut in.

'John's right,' Sarah said. 'We should get back.'

'And I am tired.' Marika stifled a yawn.

'You're not going to leave now?' Lydia looked round, aghast.

'It looks like we are, and so are you,' Sarah said firmly.

Lydia looked at Penny as if waiting for her to plead with her to stay, but Penny was staring at Roger. The pair of them didn't move.

'Don't stay up too late,' Lydia gave in gracefully. 'I'll keep an eye on Elizabeth for you, shall I, Penny?'

'Thank you,' she answered on autopilot.

'Go on then,' Roger urged when they

were finally alone.

'You want me to open it?'

'One of us has to.'

'It smells musty.' Penny sniffed the envelope.

'It's been buried for a while, I'd say.'

The envelope wasn't sealed, and Penny slid out a sheet of thick creamy paper. Carefully unfolding it, she scanned the contents.

'Well?' Roger asked.

Wordlessly, Penny handed it over.

A moment later, Roger looked up at Penny. 'Is this what I think it is?'

'If you mean Minnie's will, then yes.'

'It seems perfectly legal. I mean, it's been notarised — is that the right word?' Penny nodded. 'It's dated a year ago.'

'About the time Minnie had her first funny turn.'

'We'll have to get it properly authenticated,' Roger said, 'but I don't think that will cause a problem.'

'Did you know about this?' Penny asked.

'Of course I didn't.'

'Are you going to contest it?'

'What for? I've got half of everything.'

'And Minnie's left the other half to me,' Penny said before sinking into a chair.

# 18

'On the understanding we develop the theatre into a community centre,' Roger said in a quiet voice. 'Great minds think alike, wouldn't you say? Penny?' he prompted.

'How can Minnie have done this?'

'I expect the success of the pat-a-dog scheme gave her the idea.'

'Honestly, at times she really was the limit.' Penny paced backwards and forwards across the kitchen floor. 'What's so funny?' she snapped at Roger, who was now smiling broadly.

'Do you know, you're beginning to sound exactly like me?'

'I am not,' Penny protested.

'Yes you are,' he insisted.

'Fancy hiding a wretched will where no one would find it. I mean, come on, it's hardly the act of a grown-up. Why didn't she tell someone where she'd put it?'

'She told me,' a small voice interrupted their exchange. Elizabeth was framed in the doorway, hopping nervously from one foot to the other. 'Hello,' she said as two pairs of eyes swung in her direction.

Penny forced a smile and asked in a gentle voice, 'What exactly did Minnie say to you, Elizabeth?'

'She said — ' Elizabeth began.

'Lucetta!' an imperious voice called from the conservatory. 'Come back here at once.'

Ignoring Lydia's command, Lucetta pattered into the kitchen, and with a swish of her tail curled up in her basket by the Aga.

'You'd better come in and close the door, Elizabeth,' Penny said.

'I'm not in any trouble, am I?'

'Of course you're not,' Roger intervened. 'We're trying to work out what happened here. Now tell us what you know.'

'Minnie asked me how I liked living in the theatre and I said I loved it and I would like to live there for ever and ever.'

'Go on,' Penny urged her daughter.

'Minnie said she had a secret piece of paper in her special tin, and that she was going to put it in a hiding place at the back of the chimney for safe keeping. She didn't want everyone to know about it, but she said it would be all right if I told you.'

'And?' Penny prompted when Elizabeth fell silent.

'I forgot.' Elizabeth's face was a picture of misery.

'No harm done.' Penny stroked her daughter's fringe out of her eyes.

'Does this mean we can stay for ever and ever?' Elizabeth asked, a hopeful look in her blue eyes.

'There are things Roger and I need to discuss.'

'I don't mind if you and Roger want to get married,' Elizabeth said, 'like Marika and John. I could be a bridesmaid and I could teach Roger how to groom Bracken properly.'

A silence fell in the kitchen. 'Why don't you go and join the others?' Penny eventually suggested.

'All right.' A disconsolate Elizabeth trailed out of the kitchen, followed by an inquisitive Lucetta.

Penny turned back to face Roger. 'What do you think we ought to do?'

'We could take your daughter's advice and live here for ever and ever.'

'I thought you wanted to sell the property.'

'I don't think there will be much demand for a run-down cottage with a hole in the roof and half a chimney.'

'Are we sure the document's legal?'

'I'll have it checked out, but it looks the business to me.'

'Why didn't Minnie consult a solicitor and do it properly?'

'Perhaps she thought they might try to talk her out of it.'

'And what about the developers?'

'What about them?'

'Haven't they got first call on the land?'

'You'd have to speak to Lydia about that one.'

'Lydia.' Penny smacked a hand to her forehead. 'Someone's going to have to break the news to her.'

'I already know. Elizabeth left the door open.' Lydia was now standing in the doorway with a self-satisfied smile on her face.

'Is everyone out there eavesdropping on our private conversation?' Roger asked.

'Yes,' Lydia replied. 'By the way, if anyone wants my opinion, I'm on your side with the community centre thing. I never wanted the wretched land in the first place.'

'You didn't?' Penny echoed.

'When Minnie was alive, I pretended I did just to get back at her and Liam. I know it was immature of me. There was never anything between the pair of them. Like all artists, Liam was vain, but we both knew he and Minnie would have driven each other mad.' Lydia held out her arms. 'If you want my approval, you have it. Go ahead — you have my full permission to do anything you like with the land, as long as you don't sell it to developers and make a hideous profit.'

'We'd have to make it legal,' Penny insisted.

'Of course. I've got no hidden paperwork stuffed up my chimney so I won't make things difficult for you. But I would like an invitation to the wedding.'

'What wedding?' Penny asked.

'Don't you realise that was Minnie's real plan?'

'I don't follow.' Penny shook her head.

'That was why she didn't make a proper will. Don't you see? She wanted to delay things so you two could get to know each other better. She was a crafty old thing.'

'You've lost me,' Roger admitted.

'For goodness sake, can't you see it?' Lydia now directed her question at

Penny. 'She loved you and she loved Roger, and she wanted the two people she most loved in this world to marry. It's as simple as that. And if the pair of you haven't realised what she was up to, then I despair. Now, I'm going back to join the others. Don't take all night about proposing, Roger, because John and Sarah want to get back to The King's Head before sunrise. Ask John to give you some tips about popping the question if you're stuck on how to go about it.'

'That's outrageous.' Penny swung round and nearly toppled over. 'How did you manage to cross the room so fast?' she asked as she collided with Roger.

'I did it while you weren't looking,' he confessed.

'What are you doing now?' Penny put her hands on his chest in an attempt to push him away.

'I'm going to kiss you,' Roger said, 'and then in accordance with everyone's instructions, I'm going to ask you to marry me.'

'Hang on a moment,' Penny protested.

'Now what?' Roger asked with a pained expression on his face.

'Supposing I don't accept.'

'Then I'll have to keep on kissing you until you do,' Roger replied. 'Any more objections?'

'Lydia's boundaries?'

'You heard what she's got to say on the matter.'

'Bracken?'

'He's my new best friend, and Elizabeth's going to teach me how to groom him.'

'You don't like dogs.'

'I've outgrown my phobias, like Alice. Good, isn't it? Result all round.'

'You'd inherit a ready-made family.'

'You mean Elizabeth? I'm sure I could bribe her with the promise of chocolate biscuits for tea.'

'Hooray!' A little voice reached them from the conservatory.

'You heard your daughter,' Roger said, laughing. 'She said hooray.'

'It would mean a lot of work,' Penny pressed. 'Community centres don't come cheap.'

'Are you going to stand there all night and make excuses?'

'I'm merely pointing out the pitfalls.'

'You know we're going to have to get married.'

'Why?' Penny was beginning to feel annoyed by Roger's highhandedness.

'You're in serious danger of getting stuffy. Minnie would be very disappointed with your lack of spirit.'

Penny blinked up at Roger. His smile cracked the last of her resolve. 'For ever and ever?' she asked in a shaky voice.

'Now you're getting the idea.' Roger tightened his hold around Penny's waist. His eyes were a reflection of Minnie's — a mixture of love and laughter. Minnie could be infuriating, and at times downright annoying; but her love was absolute, and Penny had no doubt life with Roger would be exactly the same.

'To save you the trouble of going

down on one knee,' she said in a voice she hoped wouldn't be overheard by those present in the conservatory, 'I accept your proposal.'

'Good on you,' Sarah said as she poked her head through the open kitchen window. 'You know, I may take up matchmaking for a living. I'm brilliant at it.'

'Didn't I tell you my nan said things would sort themselves out?' John joined her.

'Stop looking so smug, John,' Lydia said as she swept into the kitchen, followed by an overexcited Lucetta. 'And fetch some glasses.'

Lydia held up a bottle, and with whoops of joy everyone crowded back into the kitchen.

'Here's to Minnie!' Roger raised his voice above the hubbub.

'Minnie,' everyone chimed in, clinking their glasses together.

The last of the wind whispering through the trees echoed his toast.

We do hope that you have enjoyed reading this large print book.

Did you know that all of our titles are available for purchase?

We publish a wide range of high quality large print books including:
**Romances, Mysteries, Classics**
**General Fiction**
**Non Fiction and Westerns**

Special interest titles available in large print are:
**The Little Oxford Dictionary**
**Music Book, Song Book**
**Hymn Book, Service Book**

Also available from us courtesy of Oxford University Press:
**Young Readers' Dictionary**
**(large print edition)**
**Young Readers' Thesaurus**
**(large print edition)**

For further information or a free brochure, please contact us at:
**Ulverscroft Large Print Books Ltd.,**
**The Green, Bradgate Road, Anstey,**
**Leicester, LE7 7FU, England.**
**Tel:** (00 44) **0116 236 4325**
**Fax:** (00 44) **0116 234 0205**

## LADY EMMA'S REVENGE

### Fenella J. Miller

Lady Emma Stanton is determined to discover who killed her husband, even if it means enlisting the assistance of a Bow Street Runner. Sergeant Samuel Ross is no gentleman; he has rough manners and little time for etiquette. So when Emma and Sam decide the best way to ferret out the criminal is to pose as husband and wife, they are quite the mismatched pair. Soon, each discovers they have growing feelings for the other — but an intimate relationship across such a social divide is out of the question . . .